CHARLES WHITMAN

Death Suspended

Crime Connoisseur

CASSELL · LONDON

CASSELL & COMPANY LTD
35 Red Lion Square, London, WC1
Melbourne, Sydney, Toronto,
Johannesburg, Auckland

First published 1971

I.S.B.N. 0 304 93694 4   **197349**

F/ WHI

Printed in Great Britain by
Cox & Wyman Ltd.,
London, Reading and Fakenham.
F.970

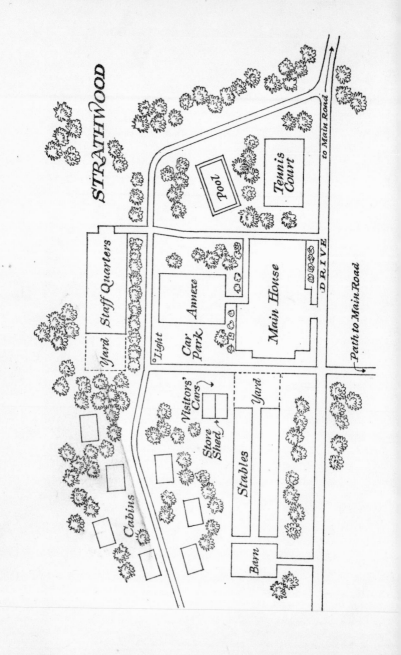

I HAVE often wondered what I would do if I became engaged on a case which proved to involve someone I knew. Contrary to legal theory which holds that a person is innocent until proved guilty a detective must assume the opposite; at least he must consider a certain number of people potentially guilty.

Naturally my thoughts on this subject were in the nature of an academic exercise since the sum total of my friends and acquaintances formed a very small proportion of the population of New South Wales and my chances of being mixed up in a case concerning any one of them extremely remote. Yet the problem had some foundation in the fact that during a case, a murder case particularly, one inevitably formed opinions about the people one met, people who could become suspects, and such opinions were necessarily coloured by one's emotional reaction to them. Whether, in fact, one liked or disliked them. It was part of the job to avoid allowing such attitudes to influence one's judgement. I sometimes wondered how difficult it would be to maintain a completely impartial relationship to people one knew personally or had met socially. In the Gwynne case I was to find out.

My connection with it began quite innocently. I ran into a girl I knew in the street one Monday morning. Detective Inspector Robert Lindon, my immediate boss, would claim that this was an all too frequent occurrence since in his opinion, a wrongly held one incidentally, I knew a damned sight too many girls. This particular girl was one I had known well in the past but whom I hadn't seen for some years. Her name was Pat Morland and she had often been my partner in mixed doubles at the White City courts. We had in fact won a few competitions together. In those days she had been about nineteen, a suntanned,

athletic blonde with a magnificent forehand drive and when I met her in Martin Place I saw with pleasure that she had grown into a very good-looking woman of twenty-three or so.

I have noticed that there is often some special attraction between people who have enjoyed what the novelists love to call shared experience but who have not met for some time, between people of the opposite sex anyway. It was good to see her and when I suggested that we might have a cup of coffee together she assented with every appearance of pleasure. Not that there had ever been anything between us other than the fun of winning or losing at tennis but it was pleasant to play some of these matches over again in retrospect, especially the winning ones. Naturally I asked her if she still played and she told me she had given up competition tennis but played occasionally at a country guest-house called Strathwood up near Castle Hill. Thus, so innocently, I moved one step nearer to murder. As a matter of fact I had heard of Strathwood, though I had never been there, because it was owned by a man I knew slightly.

'Strathwood? That's run by Alec Reeves, isn't it?' I asked Pat.

'Yes. Do you know him?'

'A little. I've bought golf clubs from him.'

Reeves had a sports goods shop in Castlereagh Street. He had been a fairly well-known athlete in his day though never quite in the top bracket in any one sport. He'd been an inter-state tennis player, a Sheffield Shield cricketer, but not a Test player, and scored in the low seventies at golf. There was little he couldn't handle competently in the sporting field. He was also quite good at making money.

'What exactly is this Strathwood place?' I asked Pat. 'I've heard mention of it occasionally but I've never quite understood what it was. A sort of country club, isn't it?'

'In a way but it's not really a club. I mean you can't

become a member, you just go and stay there as you would in a country hotel. Riding's the main attraction. Alec has some very good hacks and of course the country's ideal. So is the place itself for that matter. There's about sixty acres of it and even a race track.'

'A race track?'

Pat smiled. She looked very nice when she smiled.

'That surprises you, doesn't it? Actually it's not a proper race track but a big flat paddock fenced round in an oval with a straight stretch on one side. It has a starting gate of a kind too. The place belonged to a trainer once and he used to give his horses their preliminary training there. It's a wonderful place for riding.'

'It has a tennis court, I gather?'

'Oh yes. And a swimming pool. There's everything you need for a good week-end.'

'Sounds very nice.'

'It is. I go there a lot.'

Pat and I talked of other things for a while but I was intrigued with this Strathwood place and perhaps with Pat too. I couldn't understand what I saw in her now that I failed to appreciate years ago when we were just good tennis companions. A week-end riding, swimming and playing tennis with Pat seemed something highly desirable. But perhaps she had a regular boyfriend? She must have read my mind because she returned to the subject.

'Why don't you come up for the week-end sometime, Douglas?' she suggested. 'I'm sure you'll like it. Alec gets a very good crowd, mostly people in their twenties and thirties. He discourages teenagers, thank goodness. No long-haired guitar players or anything of that sort. There's usually a party on Saturday nights and if people want to dance there's a very good radiogram.'

'Sounds like a very good idea, Pat,' I said. 'I'm on duty some week-ends of course but . . .'

'Even policemen have a week-end to themselves

3

occasionally, don't they?'

'Oh yes. The only trouble is that if anything important breaks I could be called in, week-end or no week-end. Actually I'm free next week-end . . . if no one commits a murder.'

Pat seemed quite excited.

'Well, come then. You can drive me up.'

'That *would* be a pleasure.'

'You've changed, Douglas.'

'*I* have?'

'Yes. You never paid me compliments before. All you did was criticize my backhand.'

I grinned.

'I was too young to know what was good for me. But I will come and I'll drive you up.'

'Lovely. You do ride, don't you?'

'I was born on a horse.'

'Oh yes, I forgot. Don't you ever want to go back to the country?'

I shrugged.

'I go up occasionally. My brother Ted has the farm now that the old man has retired. I have an interest in it but it's not big enough for two to run and Ted's a better farmer than I'll ever be.'

'I can't imagine you as a farmer,' said Pat, smiling at me. 'You are much too fond of the bright lights. Incidentally, Strathwood isn't licensed. Alec is against it. He says a licence would attract the wrong sort of crowd so if you want to drink you'll have to bring your own. Most of us take a bottle. That's perfectly legal so you can leave your truncheon at home.'

'My chief weapon these days is a notebook.'

'Well, leave your notebook at home then. You won't need it at Strathwood.'

But Pat was wrong. In the end I had to use a notebook. I

4

duly went to Strathwood and ran straight into a murder though I wasn't aware of it until the week-end was almost over.

Before I left Pat that Monday morning I arranged to pick her up on Friday afternoon. Strathwood wasn't all that far away and we would be there in time for dinner. Pat would make the necessary bookings. During the rest of the week I thought quite a lot about Strathwood. It was quite a time since I had been on a horse and the thought of riding again appealed to me immensely; so, I had to admit, did the prospect of being with Pat again. I just hoped that no official duties interfered.

As it happened none did and I called for Pat at the solicitors' office where she worked a little after five on Friday. She had her suitcase and her tennis racket with her and I carried them down to my car.

'I see you are determined to get me on a court again,' I said to her as I stowed her gear in the back of the car.

'It will do you good, take some of that fat off you.'

'That's not fat, it's muscle.'

She eyed me critically.

'You are a bit heavier, Douglas. I suppose you'll be a lot slower now.'

'I'll be fast enough for you, my girl.'

'Don't kid yourself you are going to get me to play against you. I'll get Alec to take you on. He's very good. We should be able to get a decent doubles game too.'

'We'll take on all-comers.'

'All right. It'll be fun to find out whether we still play together as well as we used to.'

By this time we were in the car and I noticed with interest that Pat's long legs were still as beautifully slim as I remembered them. They hadn't developed the muscular look that so many athletic girls acquire. And her mini-skirt showed them to perfection.

We didn't say much to each other while we were leaving

5

the city. I had the peak-hour traffic to contend with and that took my attention.

'Tell me some more about Strathwood,' I said, once we were clear of the worst of the Friday night traffic.

'What do you want to know?'

'What's the food like?'

'I thought you might ask that. It's good. Nothing elaborate though. Don't imagine you're going to some chrome and gilt palace. The main building's an old country house, slightly old fashioned but full of charm and very comfortable. Cosy would be the word. I like it.'

'Cosy doesn't sound quite like you.'

'You'd be surprised. What I like is the casual atmosphere. You can wear what you like and do what you like. People have little parties in their bedrooms before dinner instead of sitting up like stuffed dummies in the lounge. In fact the lounge isn't used much except after dinner when there's dancing. What else would you like to know?'

'The accommodation?'

'Oh yes. I've booked us two rooms in the annexe.'

'Two?'

Pat's eyes widened.

'I didn't think we'd need three,' she said innocently.

'Love-fifteen,' I said. 'What's this annexe business?'

'It's a new building added to the back of the old one. The original house has only a dozen or so rooms but the annexe has twenty-four. It's modern, the bedrooms are nice and the bathrooms are better than the old ones. I thought we'd be more comfortable there.'

'Is that all the accommodation?'

'No. There are half a dozen small cottages, cabins I suppose one should call them, for married couples.'

'Only married couples?'

'Douglas, you *have* changed. You used to be so innocent.'

'That's what the police force does for one. Will the place

6

be crowded this week-end?'

'No. It's only full at holiday times. I imagine there will be somewhere between twenty and thirty, just a nice crowd.'

'And the horses? You say they are good?'

'They are. Not the usual riding-school hacks and they're well looked after.'

'I must say you paint a very pleasant picture. Looks as if we might have a very nice week-end.'

Pat smiled at me across the car.

'I see no reason why we shouldn't,' she said, somewhat cryptically. I suppose she meant that our enjoyment depended on what we did together and that opened up some interesting possibilities. We drove on in silence for a while.

My first sight of Strathwood gave me an agreeable surprise. There was a long drive between ancient trees, a whole quarter mile of it, and at the end stood the old house, single-storey and rambling in a mellow brick and faded red tiles. On the left of the drive was the racecourse, fenced with a single rail and filling most of a large flat paddock. Just before the house were the tennis court and swimming pool framed with tall trees. The light was just beginning to fade to its sunset warmth and the setting looked peaceful and nostalgic to me, a countryman born.

'Like it?' asked Pat.

'Very much indeed. If it's as good as it looks I'll be more than satisfied.'

'I knew you'd be pleased. Look, Douglas. Drive straight on and turn right to the car park, it's right next to the annexe. There's a way round the back but I'd like you to see the front of the house.'

There were a few people sitting about on comfortable chairs enjoying the last of the sunlight from beneath the trees. Some waved to Pat and she waved back.

'Most of the crowd come up on Saturday morning,' she

told me, 'so there won't be many here tonight.'

On Pat's instructions I turned right round the flank of the house. Beyond the house on my left I could see extensive stables and ahead a narrow, gravelled road with a glimpse of the cabins, placed apparently at random between the trees. I swung the car on to the car park, an open space alongside a new-looking brick building, obviously the annexe. I pulled up and switched off the motor.

'Shouldn't we have called at the house first?' I said to Pat. 'Don't we have to book in or something?'

'It isn't necessary. I told you, there's no formality here. I'm a privileged guest anyway.'

'Privileged? How come?'

'I'm not really. It's just that I've been coming here a long time on and off and I've acquired the status of a regular. I'll show you where our rooms are and then we'll go and find Alec and meet a few people.'

We carried our suitcases in, Pat leading the way. The annexe was a long building divided by a central corridor with bedrooms on either side. Ours were the last two on the right-hand side and adjacent to the bathrooms; most convenient. The rooms themselves were plain but pleasant, fitted with the usual beds, wardrobes and dressing-tables and the less usual bedside lamps. I dumped my suitcase and tennis racket and went into see Pat, pausing in the doorway of her room.

'Come in, Douglas,' she said. 'How do you like it?'

'From what I've seen so far, very good.'

'I'm glad. Don't bother to change or anything. Let's go and see what's happening. Dinner won't be very long.'

'Listen, Pat. I've got beer and whisky out in the car. Do you feel like a drink before dinner?'

'I certainly do. But leave yours where it is for the moment. Alec is sure to offer us a drink.' She paused. 'By the way, Douglas, I think I ought to tell you. Alec keeps a small stock in his office but he doesn't sell liquor except to people he knows very well. What happens is that if you run out and want a bottle he'll let you have it and put the charge on your bill as sundries. I know it's illegal and all that but . . .'

'Forget it, Pat. I'm here as plain Douglas Gray. If you like you can drop a hint to Alec that I'm blind in one eye.'

'Does he know you are a policeman?'

'Oh yes. As a matter of fact I've known him for some years very slightly. But I'm definitely not interested in policing the licensing laws.'

'Thank goodness for that. I wouldn't like there to be any awkwardness.'

'There won't. I've got enough in the car to put us both under the table for the week-end.'

'I didn't ask you up here to sponge on you, Douglas Gray,' said Pat with spirit. 'If I have some of yours you must have some of mine.'

I smiled.

'If you insist on the equality of the sexes I'll go along with you.'

'You'd better. Now let's go and find Alec and cadge a drink from him,' said Pat illogically.

We left the annexe and entered the back of the main building through a covered way decorated with pot plants. As Pat had said, there was a slightly old-world air about the house which reminded me of my parents' house in the country but it was by no means unpleasant. Quite the contrary. There seemed to be odd passages everywhere, but eventually we arrived at a largish hall from which opened a number of doors. On one side of the hall was the office. The door to the office was open but Pat knocked on it and simultaneously poked her head into the room.

'Ah, Pat,' said Alec Reeves' voice, 'come on in. Did you bring your boyfriend with you?'

'This great oaf is not my boyfriend,' Pat said, appearing

9

to give the lie to her statement by taking me by the hand and leading me into the room. 'He claims to be able to ride a horse so I thought I'd bring him up and make him prove it.'

I shook hands with Reeves, a man of forty but still with the lean toughness of the athlete. He recognized me.

'Glad you came,' he said cordially. 'It's nice to have one's old customers turning up. How's the golf?'

'Oh, so-so.'

'Douglas is an old doubles partner of mine,' Pat said. 'Of course I had to carry him most of the time but we managed to win occasionally.'

'In that case we'd better organize a game. We wouldn't have enough players for a tournament but there are one or two people who might be able to give you two a run for it.'

'What about you, Alec?'

'If I can find the time I'd be delighted. Now what about a little drink?'

So we had a drink with Reeves and we were joined a little later by a young married couple, Anne and Peter Randall, who were also regular visitors. Shortly after this we went into dinner.

Pat and I had a small table to ourselves, probably a concession to Pat's status as a regular. Although I didn't realize its usefulness at the time, this fact, coupled with the table's comparative isolation in a corner of the dining-room, enabled me to gain a comprehensive picture of the guests, Pat pointing people out to me and naming them. Actually on the Friday night this didn't mean very much since there were comparatively few guests but it was a different matter on Saturday when everyone who later featured in the drama was present.

After dinner Pat and I played a chatty game of bridge with the Randalls but we stopped after a few rubbers as Pat wished to go to bed early. We were going riding together on Saturday morning and she claimed she wanted to be fit. Fortunately I had brought a book with me so I was happy to turn in early too.

Pat was looking very healthy on Saturday morning with her smooth blonde hair and brown skin; early bed had apparently paid off. She was also looking extremely elegant in her riding kit, it suited her trim figure. We had had an early morning swim together and that had given an edge to my appetite so I felt in good form myself. We strolled down to the stables soon after breakfast. Pat had chosen my horse for me and of course her own. Mine was a big bay gelding, a very handsome animal.

'His name is Corsair,' Pat told me. 'He's an ex-racehorse.'

'Corsair? Sounds as if he might be lively.'

'No, he's not. Quite the reverse, he's very lazy. But if you can persuade him to go you'll have your work cut out to hold him. The name comes from Pirate out of Courtesan.'

'What happened to him? What is he doing as a hack?'

'He broke down, I think. Several of the horses here were racehorses once. They make lovely hacks for people who can really ride; they move so beautifully.'

Saddles were dumped beside the boxes and bridles hung over the half-doors. Pat explained that there was a groom and a stable-boy to saddle and bridle horses for people who simply regarded the animals as transport and knew little about the gear that made riding them possible but the experts, which presumably included Pat and myself, preferred to do their own chores.

'Where's your own horse?' I asked her.

'You wait till you see her. She's a beauty.'

Pat opened the door of the next box, carried the bridle in and slid it expertly over the head of a black mare. She buckled the straps and led the mare out for my inspection.

She *was* a beauty.

'There she is,' said Pat proudly. 'Midnight. Not a vice in her make-up and she'll canter on a threepenny bit.'

We saddled up. Pat mounted Midnight and I paused in tightening Corsair's girth to look at her. A good-looking girl on a good-looking horse is something to see, in my opinion, and the pair of them made a wonderful picture; the graceful blonde girl and the gleaming black mare.

'You look even better on a horse than you did on the tennis court,' I told her.

She smiled, obviously pleased.

'You've never told me before that I looked good on a tennis court.'

'I was too dazzled by your play,' I grinned.

Pat poked her tongue out at me as I checked the girth, adjusted the stirrups and threw a leg over Corsair. He moved forward delicately as I did so and then stood while I settled myself in the saddle. I patted his neck.

Pat looked across at me.

'I believe you have been on a horse before,' she said.

'Just a country boy. Where are we bound for?'

'We'll go out through the back gate. There's a whole network of soft roads and some nice open country if you want a gallop.'

The ride was extremely pleasant. It was one of those early summer days in December when the sun wasn't too hot. We had a gallop over a big paddock and I managed to persuade Corsair out of his gentle lethargy. It was exhilarating to feel his great muscles working under me and for once I missed the country. We got back to Strathwood in time for a shower, a quick swim and a peaceful beer under the trees before lunch. During the morning the week-end guests had arrived in force and the dining-room was fairly crowded when we entered it just after one o'clock. Everyone seemed to know Pat and I collected some interested glances, no doubt in the status of Pat's new boyfriend. The crowd consisted of people largely of my own age group but there was a fair sprinkling of what apeared to be young married couples and a few older men and women. Dress was casual, the atmosphere bright and cheerful, conversation animated and the scene typical of a holiday resort.

A detective acquires the habit of observation and though I took no more interest in my fellow guests than the occasion demanded, I automatically scanned the dining-room from my vantage point in the corner. Naturally I took a good look at the female element; I would find myself dancing with some of them that evening. Pat mentioned a few names which I tried to remember but it wasn't very long before a particular woman caught my eye. She was the sort of creature that invites attention.

Of course in almost every group one finds the thorough-going extrovert, 'the life of the party'. Usually it's a male and more often than not a damned nuisance but this one was a female, aged around thirty with a penetrating voice and theatrical gestures. She sat at a table in the centre of the room with a man I supposed to be her husband and the Randalls. Pat noticed the direction of my gaze and looked slightly amused.

'Isobel Gwynne,' she said. 'That's her husband Neville next to her.'

'Regular visitors?' I asked.

'Yes. But keep your eye on your lunch. Isobel has the idea she's a real man-killer.'

I grinned.

'*Is* she?'

'She tries hard enough.'

'Puss, puss, puss . . .'

'No. I'm not being catty. Isobel models herself on Bette Davis, or Tallulah Bankhead or someone . . . you know, a gay, inconsequent, don't-give-a-damn-for-anyone attitude. She drinks heavily, smokes all the time and if there are men around she simply has to show them what an intriguing personality she has.'

Mrs Gwynne was a smallish, slimly-built woman, dark-haired and good-looking in a slinky sort of way. She wore a slack suit of brilliant scarlet silk, very tight over her breasts and hips and flared widely at her ankles, a much too dressy outfit for a casual holiday lunch. As I watched her she took a cigarette from a gold pack, lighted it with a gold lighter and smoked with affected abandon.

'A sexy type?' I said.

Pat grimaced.

'Probably a tease but she gets the men in . . . some of them.'

In a way that suggests an individual knows when some-body is talking about them, Isobel Gwynne looked up and caught my eye. She had been talking, dominating the con-versation at her table apparently when she saw me but instead of looking away she gave me a sharp stare and lifted her eyebrows slightly. I wasn't quite sure what that meant, if it meant anything.

It was ten minutes later when lunch was almost over that an incident occurred that tended to bear out at least part of Pat's estimate of the Gwynne woman's character. The bright red costume was at the edge of my range of vision so I was conscious of the colour without actually looking in its direction. I saw her move and stand up. Her husband started to rise also but with an imperious gesture she put a hand on his shoulder and pushed him back in his seat. It wasn't a friendly 'don't bother to rise' gesture and Neville Gwynne looked momentarily annoyed. Never-theless he remained seated as his wife moved away from the table. She came towards Pat and me. On the way she passed another table at which was sitting a man whose name Pat had given me as Duncan Scott. I wasn't sure at the time whether Scott believed Isobel Gwynne was coming to speak to him but something passed between them as she skirted his table. He moved slightly, as if about to rise and follow her, but she brushed him off with a quick toss of her head and continued on her way. Gwynne, I noticed, was frowning after her.

She came to our table and I stood up.

'Oh, sit down,' she said to me. 'You're too damned big.' She gave me a dazzling smile to nullify her rudeness. She looked at Pat.

'How are you, Pat,' she said then, archly, 'aren't you going to introduce me?'

I thought Pat might be irritated but she just smiled.

'Mrs Gwynne . . . Douglas Gray,' she said briefly.

'Ah, Douglas. I'm Isobel. This is your first time here, isn't it?'

'Yes. But I've heard a great deal about it.'

'I'll bet you have. But don't let Pat monopolize you. We can do with some new men around here. Can't we, Pat?'

'Douglas is hardly new to me. I've known him for years.'

'Like that, is it?' She smiled at me again. 'I hope to see more of you, Douglas. Have fun.'

She gave me a look which I supposed was intended to be pregnant with meaning only I wasn't sure what the meaning was. I sat down as she walked away.

'I see what you mean,' I said to Pat.

'That was only a preliminary reconnaissance. If she thinks you might be interesting enough she'll cultivate you.'

'I wasn't given a chance to get a word in.'

'Isobel isn't interested in listening.'

'Her husband didn't look particularly happy.'

'One of these days Neville is going to clip her smartly behind the ear, though I must admit he hasn't shown much sign of doing so so far.'

We didn't pursue the subject any further and talked of other things until Alec Reeves came over to our table, doing his duty as our host.

'Everything all right?' he asked.

'Fine,' we both said.

'How did Corsair go?' Alec asked me. 'Did you get him moving?'

'Oh yes. He gallops beautifully once he understands you insist on it.'

'You've done a lot of riding then?'

'I was born on a farm. I was on a horse just as soon as I could walk.'

'Corsair would be just your cup of tea then.' Alec paused. 'What I came over to ask you was whether you'd care for a game of tennis this afternoon? I can snatch a couple of hours off duty if you'd like to play.'

'Are you issuing a challenge, Alec?' smiled Pat.

Reeves smiled back.

'I know how good you are, but if I can persuade Beryl Edwards to partner me we'll give you a run for your money.'

'It's a bet,' said Pat. 'Is that all right with you, Douglas? Or would you rather go riding again this afternoon?'

'Tennis, I think. We can ride again tomorrow.'

'Good,' said Alec. 'We'll have a couple of bottles of beer on the result. Do I book Corsair for you tomorrow, Douglas? Or would you like to try some other horse? We have some other good ones.'

'No. Corsair suits me fine.'

'Don't forget I want Midnight,' said Pat quickly.

'You know I wouldn't dream of giving Midnight to anyone else while you are here, Pat.'

'Thanks, Alec. Straight after breakfast.'

'Right. See you on the court then. I'll just make sure Beryl will play.'

At three o'clock we were on the tennis court and knocking up preliminary to the match. News of the impending battle had spread through the house and a few of the less energetic guests had gathered round the court to watch us. I felt clumsy and awkward and I knew it was going to take me a while to get my eye in. In fact Pat and I began badly, largely through my inability to get my timing right. I served a couple of double faults in my first service game and that didn't help. Pat was in trouble too. Beryl Edwards proved to be one of those awkward players to deal with. She seldom hit the ball hard and stayed safely on the baseline but she got everything back. She was a scooper, standing well back and taking the ball late after its bounce and almost ladling it over the net. But her anticipation was good and she never failed to make a return. Though these returns were easy to deal with, their very monotony forced both Pat and me into errors.

Alec, despite his forty years, was still a very good player so it wasn't very long before Pat and I were down one-four. As we changed over at the end of a game I spoke to Pat.

'Try chopping your forehand and cutting your backhand.'

She nodded and I moved up to the net.

Beryl was serving. Her first was a moderately fast, straightforward ball into the centre of the court. Pat took it in style, cutting her racket sharply under the ball without sacrificing too much of her drive. It shot low across the net, landed short and stood up in a vertical bounce against the back spin. Beryl scooped at it but the back spin fooled her. She got the end of her racket to it but it sailed over the sideline. Pat grinned at me as I dropped back to take Beryl's next service.

Pat's successful shot broke the spell. I put my return at Alec's feet and he could do nothing with it. Love-thirty. Pat took Beryl's next service on her backhand, cutting hard across Beryl's forehand. Again Beryl managed to get her racket to it but the ball was going away fast and low so she muffed the shot. Love-forty. I was now feeling a little more confident and my return of Beryl's next service cut straight between Alec and Beryl leaving them flat-footed. Game to Pat and me.

We had made our run a little late though and our opponents took the set six-four, Alec making a tremendous effort to hold the lead. The next set was very different. I started by serving a couple of aces and that set the seal on my recovery. As often happens, when one player in a doubles team finds form the other tightens up also. Pat now began to show the skill that made her such a good partner years ago, varying her chopping and cutting with sizzling cross-court drives. We quickly ran to a three-love lead.

About this time I noticed Isobel Gwynne, who had been sitting on the grass outside the court with Duncan Scott, suddenly stand up and walk away. We were changing ends and I had time to watch but what drew my attention in the first place was the quick way Isobel got to her feet and stalked off; as if something had annoyed her. The lady was given to impetuous actions apparently. Then, to my surprise, Scott also got to his feet and marched off after Isobel. They disappeared between the trees beyond the pool and I returned my attention to the game.

Pat and I now found our old form. We won the second set six-two. Actually we had started out to play an unspecified number of sets in a friendly game but as we were now one set all we decided to play the final set for the match ... and the beer. It was a good tussle but Pat finished it with a beautiful forehand drive which Alec put straight into the net. This gave us the victory, two sets to one. Together Pat and I rushed to the net to shake hands with our opponents in traditional fashion and as we reached it I put my arm round Pat's waist. When we had been regular partners I had often done this and it had been regarded by both of us as nothing more than a friendly gesture. The fact that I had been a male and Pat a female hadn't intruded; we were tennis partners at the end of an exciting game. I hadn't bothered to reason that I wouldn't have put my arm round a man's waist but on the court at Strathwood Pat's femaleness affected me like an unexpected electric shock. Her body was soft, yet firm and alive under her thin tennis dress. Pat must have felt something too because she gave me a faintly surprised look before reaching out to shake hands with Beryl.

The game over, Alec went off and came back with a couple of bottles of beer and some glasses and we sat on comfortable chairs under the big tree between the house and the tennis court to fight the match over again. The scene was incredibly peaceful. A couple of girls had taken over the tennis court and were swiping the ball backwards and forwards across the net in long, evenly-matched rallies. A few people were in the pool and a group of novice riders were trotting gently round the race track. But there was an undercurrent of something or other, a mild tension I suppose one could call it, between Pat and me which had begun on the tennis court. I guessed it could only be resolved in one way and I'm sure Pat knew it too because she occasionally glanced at me as if seeing me for the first time and when I returned her look she dropped her eyes with a faint, but knowing smile.

We sat talking and drinking until it was time to shower and change before dinner. Pat and I left together. The long corridor down the centre of the annexe was deserted. I put an arm round Pat and we walked towards our rooms in silence. At Pat's door we stopped and Pat turned inside my encircling arm and I kissed her. Then I kissed her again. She pushed me gently away.

'I think you'd better go and have a cold shower, Douglas,' she said. She reached up and kissed me quickly. 'And the way I feel, I'd better have one too.'

I left her reluctantly and later wandered into the shower room thinking deeply about biochemistry. What was it that had happened to Pat and me during the intervening years since I had last seen her that now caused us to be so acutely aware of one another in a sexual sense? I didn't know and perhaps I didn't care, I was happy enough that it had. I felt very fit after our tennis and actually sang under the shower, which wasn't normally a habit of mine since I have a voice reminiscent of a portable band-saw. Then after a brief and breathless minute under a stream of cold water, I towelled myself vigorously and opened the bathroom window to let out the steam. Because the bathrooms were at the very end of the annexe I looked out on a pleasantly rural scene. I could see the end of the staff headquarters, a building well behind the annexe, screened by trees, and the beginning of the path leading to the cabins. This path was more or less an extension of the gravel drive leading from the main drive to the car park and was the route taken by people who occupied the cabins to and from the main building. As I looked I saw Isobel Gwynne coming along the path towards the annexe and supposed, correctly as it turned out, that she and her husband occupied one of the cabins. She was some distance away from me but near enough, I thought, to recognize me through the bathroom window if she looked in my direction so I ducked out of sight.

After what Pat had told me about her I half expected some approach from her simply because I was new to the place and to that extent a challenge but she had left Pat and me severely alone, to my relief. No doubt there were other men who occupied her attention for the moment. Being not only curious about my fellow creatures but trained in the habit of observation I couldn't help taking a quick peep at her. She wore a simple mini-dress of turquoise blue; she appeared to favour bright colours. Actually she wasn't bad looking, she had nice legs, a good figure, slim with small firm breasts. It was her manner which irritated, not her looks. Evidently she didn't ride, play tennis or do anything energetic like swimming in the pool; men must be her main interest in life. As if to confirm this judgement a man appeared right on cue, walking towards her on the pathway with the obvious intention of speaking to her.

It was a man named Rodney Fuller, a pleasant sort of bloke a few years younger than Isobel. I wondered where he had come from and where he was going as the pathway was one used exclusively by the cabin dwellers and his room was in the annexe. He must, I decided, be on his way to meet or call on Isobel. At any rate he stopped, facing her, a move that didn't seem to please her particularly as she made a tentative attempt to pass him. She wasn't successful and they began to talk. I was too far away to hear what was said but their actions suggested they were not having a friendly chat about the weather, or a friendly chat about anything. Isobel was somewhat dramatic in her way of speaking. She had a high-pitched, rather loud voice, the effect of which she underscored with flamboyant gestures, as if she was proud of her hands and wanted to display them like a Balinese dancer. Fuller was evidently arguing with her about something and moving towards her but she kept backing away as if he were a nuisance. Intrigued, I kept watching. The argument, if it was an argument, came to a head. Fuller moved forward and reached out as if to take her in his arms but she avoided him and pushed him away sharply. She said something I only just failed to hear. It sounded very like, 'don't be bloody silly'.

Fuller stood still, his face set, as Isobel walked away towards the back of the annexe. As she did so, she drew nearer to me but before I ducked hurriedly out of sight I noticed her expression. It was thoroughly smug. I waited until I was sure she was out of sight and then took another look at Fuller. He was standing where she had left him, looking grim and angry. Then he took the path towards the car park and passed from my sight.

Pat was standing at the door to my room as I left the bathroom. She was fully dressed.

'My God, you men talk about the time we women spend in the bathroom . . .'

'I was looking at the view.'

She looked at me suspiciously.

'Did you have to study it from the bathroom?'

'As a matter of fact this particular view was only visible from the bathroom window.'

'Who was she?'

'Your dear little friend Isobel.'

'Oh? What was she doing that interested you so much? Sunbathing in the nude or something?'

'I regret to say she wasn't. She was having a row with Rodney Fuller. At least it looked like a row.'

Pat sniffed.

'That isn't surprising. He's one of her discards.'

'Discards? Just what does that mean? Was there anything serious between them?'

Pat stood in the doorway and talked to me as I finished dressing.

'If by serious you mean sexual, I don't know. Isobel makes a pet of a man for a while and then dumps him for someone else. How far she goes is difficult to say but Rodney got tossed aside for Duncan Scott and I fancy Duncan wouldn't waste too much time on her unless she was willing to hop into bed. One can never be certain of course but knowing Duncan I should say that she came good, as they say.'

'Are you speaking from experience?'

Pat smiled.

'Why should that interest you?' she said. 'You're just my tennis partner.'

'If you think that's all I'm good for I'll show you . . .'

Pat backed away in mock fright.

'Save your strength, Douglas,' she said quickly. 'I don't care for Duncan Scott.'

'He didn't impress me either but what does Neville

Gwynne have to say about all this? Does he let her get away with it?'

'Apparently. But a husband can be the last person to know. Isobel's a cunning little devil and the opportunities are plentiful in a place like this. Everybody here is aware that she has been encouraging Duncan but I get the impression that Neville thinks that it's nothing but feminine exhibitionism and heaven knows she indulges in plenty of that.'

'Could this exhibitionism be a cover for a little sexual indulgence with whoever is available?'

'I think she's just a tease. Flamboyant creatures like her often are.'

'You are probably right. All the same her husband must be a spineless sort of creature.'

'Oh the worm will turn, one of these days.'

'You think so? What could he do? He can hardly keep her locked up.'

'I know what I'd do if I were Neville.'

'What?'

'Put her across my knee and give her bottom a damned good smacking, her bare bottom, for preference.'

I grinned.

'Do you think that would work?'

'I think it's just what she needs. All Neville has to do is to assert himself just once. At present she holds him in contempt because she keeps getting away with it and she'll go on getting away with it until Neville says that's enough.'

'Maybe you're right. Where are we bound for now?'

'The Randalls. We'd better take a bottle though. Whisky, I think.'

'I've got some here.'

'So have I.'

'We'll take mine.'

'No mine. It's my turn. You can produce yours after dinner.'

23

DINNER that night was a lively affair. The few drinks Pat and I had had with the Randalls had put us into a cheerful frame of mind and the same seemed to be true of the rest of the guests with one notable exception. This was the table at which Isobel and Neville Gwynne sat. The dining-room was fairly full as a number of visitors had arrived for dinner and the evening's festivities so Isobel's frowning countenance showed in marked contrast to the otherwise congenial atmosphere. She must have been in a foul temper. Pat was unable to see her but every time I turned my head I got a grandstand view and noticed how rude to her husband she appeared to be.

I wondered whether some telepathic communication had reached Neville from Pat and he had at last taken Isobel firmly in hand but if so it hadn't had the desired effect for she was certainly not eating out of his hand. Quite the contrary. The Randalls were doing their best to lower the temperature and getting snubbed for their pains. Or so it seemed to me from a distance.

'It looks as if it might be a good party tonight, Douglas,' Pat said. 'You're going to be dragged on to the floor if I have to get a crowbar to shift you.'

'All right,' I said resignedly. 'No cha-cha though.'

She laughed aloud.

'That *would* be something to see.'

'Well, you're not going to see it. I will dance with you though . . . if you're good.'

'Good? You'd better dance with me or I'll refuse . . .'

Pat stopped and actually blushed a faint pink, adding a touch of warmth to her suntanned skin.

'You'll refuse what?' I asked her.

'I think you know what I meant. If you don't you must be slower witted than usual.' She smiled at me across the table. 'The whisky must have gone to my head.'

'Good,' I grinned.

'That's enough, Douglas. Keep your mind on your food,' she added unfairly. 'There's a good crowd here to-night.'

Later, after coffee, the lounge was cleared for dancing. Somebody put some records on the radiogram and the party began. I danced with Pat and sundry other females without actually breaking anyone's toes. Pat was pleased with me.

'You're a fraud, Douglas,' she accused. 'You can dance quite well when you set your mind to it.'

By this time the guests had settled into small, separate groups, ours including the Randalls and a mixed bunch of young unmarrieds. The Gwynnes were not in evidence, which surprised me as Isobel was supposed to be a confirmed party girl. Curiously both Duncan Scott and Rodney Fuller were absent also.

Part of this mystery was cleared up during the evening when I was dancing with Anne Randall. I remarked that dinner must have been something of an ordeal for her and Peter.

'It was dreadful,' Anne said. 'I've never seen Isobel in such an irritating mood.'

'It's a bit unlike her to miss a night like this, isn't it?'

Anne smiled up at me. She was rather a small girl but beautifully made and a very good dancer.

'That was just the trouble. Neville had to drive into town and pick up someone at Mascot, some very important client, I gathered. He thought Isobel should go with him and help entertain the client for the evening but she wasn't at all keen on the idea. She said that all Neville's clients were dreary old men and she didn't see why she should give up an evening's fun to drive all that way and do Neville's dirty work for him. A bit unfair of her, I thought.'

'Well, she's not here so Neville must have won the

argument in the end.'

'He must have put his foot down for once.'

I didn't think any more about Isobel until her name came up about twelve o'clock on Sunday morning. The Saturday night party didn't end until about one o'clock but Pat and I were up reasonably early for a morning's riding. This time we joined a few other people to ride over the rolling country to the north of Strathwood. The weather was still fine and we got back about twelve, ready for a pleasant beer before lunch. We also got back to find a buzz of excitement running through the house. Neville Gwynne had returned from town, arriving at Strathwood at about ten-thirty, had gone to his cottage and then wandered over to the main house asking casually if anyone knew where his wife was.

Alec Reeves gave Pat and me the story, as distinct from the rumours, just before we went into lunch.

'I was in the hall when Neville turned up,' Alec said. 'He'd been to the cottage, dumped his bag, and had come over to the house looking for Isobel. He wasn't worried, he just asked if I or anyone else knew where she was. Isobel doesn't ride very often so he expected to find her somewhere handy. Naturally I was very surprised. I said I was under the impression that she had left with him on Saturday night as she hadn't been seen since that time.'

'She hadn't gone with Neville then?'

'No.'

'Just when did he leave?' I asked.

'Straight after dinner as far as I know. He was to go to Mascot, pick up some client of his, take him to a hotel and then entertain him for the evening.'

'Yes, I know that. But I thought Isobel refused to go.'

'That's what Neville says. Apparently they had a bit of an argument about it at dinner and were still arguing up to the time Neville left. He said she went out to the car with him and they had a last-minute quarrel until Neville told

26

her he had to go. He admits he got a bit fed up with her refusal to behave reasonably and finally drove off leaving her standing on the car park.'

'But where could she have got to then?' asked Pat.

Alec shook his head.

'I'm damned if I know. It's a puzzle. And I don't care for its implications very much either.'

The three of us were alone, standing under the big tree by the tennis court, which was now deserted.

'Why not, Alec?' I asked.

He frowned.

'Running a place like this is not as simple as it sounds. I know what goes on here but it's my policy not to interfere in guests' private affairs providing they don't affect other people's enjoyment. I'm quite aware that in a free and easy place like this somebody occasionally ends up in someone else's bed. This is inevitable but if people are discreet about it I don't see that it's any business of mine.'

'What are you getting at, Alec?'

'Neville is inclined to believe that Duncan Scott took Isobel away somewhere and spent the night with her.'

'Has he any grounds for believing that?'

'It's hard to say. Neville's not insistent on it but he believes that is what happened.'

'It doesn't look very good, I must say. I haven't seen Scott around since dinner last night.'

'That's just the trouble, Douglas. Duncan left last night.'

'Left Strathwood altogether?'

'Yes. Straight after dinner.'

'But why? Did he say?'

'No. And I don't ask questions. He came to me just before seven and said he'd decided to go back to town. He paid his bill and as far as I know left immediately. As a matter of fact, knowing something of what has been going on I assumed that he'd had a row with Isobel. He seemed a bit upset.'

'Seven o'clock? That's about the time Neville left, isn't it?'

'I think he got away a bit earlier than that but I'm not certain.'

'So Scott *could* have picked Isobel up and taken her away?'

Alec nodded.

'That's what I don't like. You see if Isobel had had a row with Neville on the car park she might have gone off with Duncan in a huff and spent the night with him. She's mad enough for that. As far as I am concerned that's their business but if it's true and Neville does something about it I could be in for some unpleasant publicity. These week-ends only just pay. The time I really make money is during holiday times; in fact the place is full of families and kids right through the school holidays. The point is that women are not going to bring their kids here if the place gets a bad reputation.'

I could appreciate Alec's position. A divorce action, if it came to that, would not only bring unwelcome attention in itself but would result in publicity about Isobel's activities in general. She was exactly the type to interest newspaper reporters looking for a juicy story. But the assumption that she had gone off with Duncan Scott was hardly justified yet. I pointed out to Alec that there wasn't any real evidence. But he was still worried.

'I don't know, Douglas,' he said. 'It seems highly suspicious that Scott went to the car park, as I presume he did, just at the time when Isobel was expected to be there. It could have been an arrangement between them. On the other hand, as I said, Isobel is just the sort of madcap to do something stupid like persuading Scott to take her away.'

'But would Scott have agreed to that? He must have

known that nothing but trouble could result from it.'

'I really don't know. But the fact is that Isobel has gone somewhere and the most likely explanation is that she has gone with Scott.'

As it was now nearly lunchtime Alec had to go and our conversation ended. There were several things I had wanted to ask him but only to satisfy my curiosity. Isobel's affairs were no concern of mine. If Alec needed advice he could talk to me later. Naturally, I discussed the matter with Pat over lunch, in common with the rest of the guests. This was the kind of event people love talking about, especially in the relaxed atmosphere of a holiday guest-house where everyone was grouped together much as on shipboard. Budding romances were quickly recognized and plenty of guesses made as to how far they had gone. No doubt Pat and I had furnished some raw material for rumours. Neville wasn't in to lunch and I heard later that Alec had sent a tray over to his cabin.

Alec, passing through the dining-room, stopped and told us that Neville was now convinced that Isobel had gone off with Duncan Scott and was talking about rushing off to Sydney to confront them. Alec dissuaded him, pointing out sensibly that Neville didn't know where they were and if Isobel had decided to leave him it was useless to go looking for her. If she hadn't she would probably turn up later with some sort of explanation.

Pat suggested that I ought to do something.

'No, Pat,' I said firmly. 'I am not here in any official capacity and in any case it's not a police matter if Isobel has really gone off with Scott. I can't barge in on people's private affairs.'

'You are a detective. You could help Neville to find out whether she has or not.'

'I can do that only by asking questions. By finding out whether anyone, either amongst the guests or the staff, saw her getting into Scott's car. That sort of thing. But that's something I just can't do in the circumstances.'

'No . . . I suppose not.'

'All the same there are one or two things I would like to know, just out of curiosity.'

'What things, Douglas?'

'Well, for a start, the very obvious question of whether Isobel took all her clothes away with her.'

'Good Lord, yes. How silly. Let's go and ask Alec, he might know.'

'No,' I said quickly. 'I don't want to be involved. I don't mind talking to you about it but I simply can't interfere otherwise.'

'I suppose you're right, Douglas. Sorry.'

I smiled at her.

'Don't let your enthusiasm for detection run away with you. Neville should be able to work that one out for himself. Obviously if her clothes are gone she has gone . . . probably for good.'

'I feel certain she went off deliberately, whether she took her clothes or not.'

'Why?'

'Isn't it obvious? She knew Neville would be away all night. If all she wanted was to go to bed with Duncan she could have done so without leaving Strathwood.'

'Well, we don't know but the absence of her clothes would be a strong pointer. The second thing I'd like to know is just how true it is that she had been having an affair with Duncan.'

Pat frowned.

'I think *that's* fairly certain.'

'But you're guessing really. Having a mild flirtation is one thing but for a married woman to go to bed with another man is a rather different matter. My point is that the evidence for each is much the same. Unless they were actually caught in a compromising situation no one is likely to know just how far the thing had gone.'

'I suppose not. Isobel just *looks* as if she'd end up in bed.'

'Another thing I'd like to know is what sort of relationship Neville and Isobel had. Some married couples allow one another a fair amount of latitude when it comes to casual affairs with the opposite sex. Did Neville ever give any indication that he resented Isobel's behaviour? I have the impression he took it all rather meekly. Just how true is that?'

'How does one know, Douglas? Neville seemed to regard Isobel's behaviour as mere fun but I don't know what took place between them in private. I have an idea money played some part in it.'

'Isobel's money?'

'Yes. She has a half-share in a very successful dress shop.'

'What does Neville do?'

'He's an advertising executive. I think he has a very good job but Isobel's income could be a lot higher than his. They live very well. He drives a Jaguar and she has a Rover 2000 and you don't run cars like that on peanuts.'

'No, you don't. It's an interesting point. A lot of marriages are held together by sheer economics but it looks as if Isobel could have walked out on Neville any time she pleased.'

'Then perhaps she has.'

'Superficially it looks a bit like it but somehow the circumstances don't quite fit.'

'Why not, Douglas?'

'Well you know as well as I do that normally a woman doesn't leave her husband just on a mere whim. There's usually a long period of tension and a great deal of argument before the thing finally breaks. There are a great many practical considerations, who gets the house, who wants this and that, and so on. This looks much more like a wildly impulsive move.'

'Do you mean she might turn up again before long?'

'It wouldn't surprise me at all. I can just see her walking in as bold as brass and telling Neville she got bored and wanted to spend a night away just for fun.'

'That would be like her, I must admit.'

But Isobel hadn't turned up by the time lunch was over, nor had she by three o'clock when Alec came to talk to Pat and me. We were sitting by the pool in the sun and trying to make up our minds whether to have a game of tennis and a swim later or whether to swim first.

'Any sign of the truant?' Pat asked Alec as he dropped on to the grass beside us.

'No. She's gone off all right. I told Neville the best thing he can do is to pack up and go home. He's not doing any good moping around here.'

'Is he going?'

'No. He has some sort of hope that she might turn up.'

'Alec,' said Pat. 'Did Isobel take all her clothes with her?'

'No, she didn't.'

'She just walked out with nothing but what she was wearing?'

'Apparently.'

'Isn't that a bit puzzling?' I said. 'It's most unlike a woman to go off without taking at least a change of clothes with her. That is if she is going for good.'

'I thought so at first but Neville says not. She couldn't have packed anything while he was there; he'd have been suspicious.'

'She could have packed after he had gone.'

'Well no. The theory is that Duncan Scott picked her up on the car park and whisked her away. Scott wouldn't have wanted to hang around while Isobel packed and increase the risk of them being seen together. In any case, according to Neville Isobel had so many clothes that the loss of what she had here wouldn't have worried her a scrap. She could have collected what she needed from her home either last night while Neville was away or some time today.'

'It sounds possible,' I said. 'But tell me, Alec. You must have a fair idea of what goes on here. Do you really believe Isobel has gone off with Scott?'

'To be honest I'm damned if I know.'

'Was she serious about him?'

'Heaven only knows. I would have said that she was serious about nothing except herself.'

'The point is of course that if she had been merely having fun and games with Scott in a mild sort of way she will probably turn up again. On the other hand . . .'

'Do you think she had been sleeping with Duncan?' said Pat suddenly.

Alec looked as if he would have preferred not to have to answer the question but after a short pause he did.

'Look. As the proprietor of this guest-house I haven't any idea but as an individual I'm damned sure she had.'

'Do you have any particular reason for believing that?' I asked Alec.

He didn't answer for a while. Then he took a deep breath.

'One of the things I don't like about this business is that I happen to know what a wild bitch that woman is. She could wreck this place. I have personal experience.'

'She tried her sex appeal on you did she, Alec?' Pat asked.

'She certainly did. But for heaven's sake keep this under your hat, I don't come out of it too well myself as the owner of this place. She came to my room one night. It was a Saturday like last night, a pleasant party and no one got offensively drunk except perhaps Isobel. She was here alone. Neville had some business in town and didn't come up until Sunday and of course Isobel was having a whale of a time playing up to every man in sight and being the life of

33

the party. We finished up about one and everyone went to bed. I took a last look round and went to bed myself but I'd only just turned the light out when Isobel came into my room carrying a couple of glasses. There was enough light out in the hall for me to see who it was and what she was carrying. She told me to put the light on as she had a lovely drink for me. I put the light on but I told her I didn't want a drink, I'd had enough and so had she. She said she'd made it specially for me with ice and lemon and all the trimmings and I'd have to drink it or she would be very hurt. I told her I didn't care for gin and it was very late and she ought to be in bed and the little devil said I had very good ideas and she'd be happy to go to bed just as soon as we had finished our drinks.'

Alec paused and shook his head at the recollection.

'I was in a difficult situation. I could see she was just drunk enough to make a damned nuisance of herself and she was wearing nothing but a flimsy gown so I'd need to be extremely diplomatic to get rid of her without her making a scene.'

'Was it obvious that she had nothing on but a gown?'

'Not then, but it was later. I told her I'd take the drink if she promised to go to her own room immediately afterwards, at which she said she never made promises she couldn't keep. I asked her what her husband would think if he knew what she was doing and she said it didn't matter, he was probably in bed with some floozie anyway. In the end I took one of the drinks from her and drank it. She drank hers and I said I'd done what she'd asked and now she would have to go and if she didn't go voluntarily I'd have to put her out. That, I might tell you, was the silliest thing I could have done because she accepted it as a challenge. She slipped off the gown, let it drop to the floor and said "Are you going to throw me out like this, darling?" I knew then that I wasn't going to get rid of her but I made a stupid attempt to try and put the gown back on her and

34

that was the end of it. I'm just as susceptible to female charms as the next man and she is attractive enough even dressed. Naked, she was too much to cope with. Anyway I knew if I got as far as actually putting her out of the door she would have probably yelled her head off and brought the guests running to see what was wrong. So we ended up in bed.'

'The woman's a nymphomaniac,' said Pat. 'Did she stay with you all night?'

'Until just before it got light.'

'Do you think her behaviour that night was typical?'

'Oh God, yes. It wasn't my manly beauty that attracted her, that's for sure. If I may coin a word I think she is a nympho-egomaniac; once she sets her sights on some man she has to have him and her sights could fall on anybody. I gave you only the briefest outline of what took place. We were arguing for maybe forty minutes before I decided that it would be easier to give her what she wanted rather than have her scream the place down from injured vanity. She was perfectly capable of doing just that. It's what I meant when I said she was a wild bitch.'

'Surely Neville must have had some inkling of what she was like?'

'I don't know, Doug. He never knew she'd slept with me, I'll swear. He may have suspected her at times but she was as cunning as a snake and shrewd enough to avoid being caught in the act. My opinion is that he had some idealistic picture of her that nothing could disturb except maybe actual first-hand evidence. But Neville's an egotist in his own way and maybe he doesn't want to know she's making a damned fool of him.'

'It looks as if she really has gone off with Duncan then,' said Pat.

Alec looked gloomy.

'I don't give a damn what she's done so long as Strathwood doesn't get dragged into it. A really juicy divorce case could just about ruin me.'

'I wouldn't worry too much, Alec,' I said. 'She could turn up any minute. So far we've only talked about what Isobel might do but what about Scott? Would he have gone off with her, I wonder? A little fun and games with an attractive and co-operative female is one thing but to be tied up with a woman like that permanently is a different story.'

'You could be right but if Isobel is up to some stupid prank she's taking her time about it. It's nearly half past three and still no sign of her.'

'What's Neville doing, Alec?' asked Pat.

'When I last saw him he was sitting in his cottage looking sorry for himself. I think he's too embarrassed to face the crowd. I'll tell him he ought to go home.'

'I don't think I'd do that if I were you,' I said to Alec. 'It is still possible that Isobel will turn up. I'd give her until tonight anyway.'

I don't give myself credit for being psychic but Isobel did turn up, in most unexpected circumstances. But this was a little later. After our conversation Alec went back to the house and Strathwood settled down to a peaceful Sunday afternoon. The talking died away for want of new information and it was generally considered that Isobel had simply walked out on Neville. The next news wasn't expected until the newspapers reported a divorce action.

Pat and I had a couple of sets of tennis with the Randalls, Pat and Peter aginst Anne and me. Afterwards we had a swim and Pat and I wandered over to the annexe to change. I had a quick shower and had just got into slacks and a sports shirt when Alec came tearing down the annexe corridor and the peace of the afternoon was shattered. My door was partly open and Alec pushed his way in without ceremony but the look of strain on his face overrode any considerations of politeness.

'Douglas,' he said urgently. 'I need your help. Isobel has been found.'

I knew by his use of the word 'found' that he hadn't come to report that Isobel had walked in under her own power and the anguished look on his face made it obvious that something very unpleasant had happened to her. It didn't take much guessing what that was.

'You mean her body has been found?'

'Yes. She's dead all right. Very dead.'

Pat, whose door had also been slightly open, came rushing into my room, zipping up her dress.

'Did you say that Isobel was dead, Alec?' she asked breathlessly.

'I'm afraid so.'

'Where is she?' I asked.

'In the store shed.'

'Where's that? Over near the stables?'

'Yes.'

'Was she . . . was she murdered?' asked Pat.

Alec nodded.

'Oh yes. There isn't any doubt about that.'

This brought me right into the picture. From now on I was no longer a guest but a policeman. I would have to take charge.

'Who else knows?' I asked Alec quickly.

'Only Saunders, the handyman. He found her.'

'Did you tell him to keep his mouth shut?'

'Hell, yes. I don't want the whole damned place in an uproar. Things are bad enough as they are.'

'Let's go then.'

I started to move away with Alec, and Pat made as if to follow us.

'Stay there, Pat, please,' said Alec quickly. 'It's not a pretty sight. If you go to the house don't say a word. Douglas will have to handle this.'

'Better stay here, Pat,' I said. 'For the time being

anyway. 'I'll come back when I can.' I turned to Alec. 'This is going to be public knowledge very soon. It just can't be helped. I'll have to get a team out from Headquarters and very likely the thing will be taken out of my hands.'

'Can't you look after it? You know the place and the people.'

'I can't promise, Alec. I'll give Inspector Lindon a ring and he'll have to decide. Probably he'll come out himself but in the circumstances I may be barred from taking any active part in the investigation.'

'Come back and tell me what has happened,' Pat said.

'I'll be very busy, Pat. I'll try.'

She looked a little forlorn and I smiled to reassure her.

'I'll come back as soon as I get a moment,' I told her.

Alec and I moved off again.

'Don't hurry, Alec,' I said, as he started to stride down the corridor. 'Be as casual as you can. We don't want to attract attention.'

Alec slowed down but led the way out of the annexe and turned right to cross the front of the car park. Diagonally to our left between the stables a few people were unsaddling horses but they were a little distance away and took no notice of us. Immediately in front of us, on the other side of the narrow lane that led from the main drive to the car park and the area where the cabins were, was a large shed with two doors indicating that it was divided into two.

'What's in the store shed?' I asked Alec.

'One half contains non-perishable food and stuff we use for the house. The other half's a dump for all the odd things we don't need. Broken furniture, old saddlery and gear, boxes, crockery, timber and heaven knows what. I'm always threatening to clean it out but some of the stuff is useful and somehow I've never been able to find the time to sort it out.'

'It's not locked, I take it?'

'The store half is but the other half isn't. That's where Isobel is.'

By this time we had reached the shed but Alec stopped me before I could open the door.'

'She's been hanged, Douglas,' he said. 'That's how I knew she'd been murdered. I ought to warn you, it's a very unpleasant sight. I damned nearly spewed myself.'

'Don't worry. This won't be the first body I've seen.'

At this point we were out of sight to the people at the stables and there was no one else around. I used a handkerchief to open the door though I knew it was probably a waste of effort. Alec and the handyman had already grasped the brass knob and it would be a very careless murderer who left fingerprints. We slipped inside quickly. The light was rather dim as the single rather grubby window was partially obscured by planks of timber leaning against the wall. But the light was good enough to see what Alec had meant. Isobel was strung by the neck from one of the rafters that crossed the building about ten feet up. She was naked down as far as her ankles from which her clothes hung in a torn, untidy cascade. She had been strangled with a length of leather strap, looped about her neck and tied to the rafter above. Her face was swollen and cyanozed to a dirty blue-grey colour and crossed by a gag of grubby rag. Her sightless eyes stared in fright towards the roof and her once beautiful body showed marble white, patterned faintly with sunburn. Her arms were held behind her, evidently tied at the wrists, so that her pale breasts were thrust forward in a last, macabre appeal. Obviously she had been dead for a considerable time.

I stood a few feet from the body, my eyes and brain busy. It was easy, I thought, to reconstruct what had happened. The murderer had brought her to the shed either already gagged and tied or had kept a hand over her mouth until he had been able to gag and tie her inside. He had

39

stood her on a chair, put the strap around her neck and passed it through a buckle. He had then stood on a box, looped the strap over the rafter and tied it tightly. He had then ripped off her clothes. Her dress, the bright turquoise mini she had worn at dinner, her brassière, her panties, suspender belt and nylons were draped in a way that suggested he had torn everything from her body in an absolute fury, shreds of material remained dangling from her arms and her underclothes were ripped as if wrenched down in one mad pull. His final act was to withdraw the chair from under her so that she hung suspended from the rafter and died from strangulation. Even that last act must have been one of vicious anger for the chair was lying in front of her with threads of turquoise clinging to the roughness on its surface.

Alec was standing just behind me as I made my careful inspection. I turned to him.

'Is there a key to this place?' I asked him.

'I've got one somewhere. As I said, we don't usually bother to keep it locked.'

'Will you try and find it? I don't intend to touch anything until Inspector Lindon gets here.'

'You'll cut her down, won't you? She looks ... well when you've actually known the girl ...'

'I know how you feel but there could be important clues in little things like the way the knots are tied. And she has to be photographed.'

'Like that?'

'Better go and look for that key, Alec.'

Alec turned abruptly and left. I took a careful look at the body again, moving round it without disturbing anything. It was smooth and unmarked, as if the murderer had worked quickly and efficiently. As I had guessed, her wrists were tied together and probably her ankles were tied also but they were invisible under the mass of her torn clothes. I moved round in front of her again. I stared down at the

40

chair, overturned and lying a couple of feet in front of the body. Everything about this crime suggested that it had been done in white-hot anger by someone who had conceived a bitter hatred for Isobel. He had literally whipped the chair from under her, crashing it to the floor. No doubt he had watched her struggle and die. I gently pressed a finger against the fleshy part of her thigh. The body swayed slightly but rigidly. Rigor had not yet passed so she had probably died some time on Saturday evening. The box on which the murderer had stood was still in position beside the body. It could possibly carry dust and dirt that might help to establish his movements. I stood back and looked around the shed.

As Alec had said it was not much more than a junk room, crowded with discarded furniture, crates, torn lampshades, bed-ends, odd bits of timber and miscellaneous items. A couple of shelves held old crockery and utensils and I noticed with a sudden interest that at one end was a tangled skein of binder twine, identical with the string used to tie Isobel's wrists. Also, hooked on to the walls with sundry old bridles, curb reins and other bits of riding gear were many lengths of rein, similar to the piece used to hang Isobel. No doubt they were relics of the days of ponies and traps. One thing was clear. The murderer must have been aware that he would find all the things he needed assembled ready for use in the store shed so he must have been familiar not merely with Strathwood but with the contents of the store shed. It looked as if he had dragged or carried Isobel into the shed and bound and gagged her there. I shied away from consideration as to who might have this knowledge. It was much too early for speculation.

A FEW minutes later Alec came back with the key. Silently we left the store shed and I locked the door and pocketed the key. We walked back to the house.

'Would many of your guests know of the contents of that store shed?' I asked Alec.

He shrugged.

'It's difficult to say. Anyone who came here at all regularly would probably know.'

'It's used frequently then?'

'Fairly. The staff dump things they don't need in there and Jim Saunders, the handyman, often goes in to hunt for a bit of wood or something. It's a matter of luck. A guest might become aware of it on his first visit and on the other hand you could come here a dozen times and not know about it.'

We continued our walk to the house trying to look casual. The guests were now mostly inside taking their pre-dinner drinks or changing but the regular twang of a tennis racket hitting a ball indicated that a few people were still at play. Nobody as yet suspected that Isobel's body was hanging grotesquely not very many yards away. The point posed a problem for me.

'When do the guests start leaving as a rule?' I asked Alec.

'After dinner, generally. Some stay later, some even spend Sunday night here and go back to town early on Monday. One couple has already left.'

'Do you have their name and address?'

'Oh yes. I have everyone's.'

My problem was to prevent anyone leaving. I could probably get some men to Strathwood in half an hour but hardly any sooner. There was a small police station at Castle Hill but that was staffed only by a couple of men. I couldn't take any from there. My best bet was probably a patrol car; there were many on the road and one could be reached from Headquarters. The team from Headquarters itself could hardly reach Strathwood in less than an hour and a quarter. Although I knew that all the guests except one, and possibly all of them, were innocent, I couldn't let them go without getting statements from them. I certainly couldn't let anyone go until I knew just when Isobel had died.

The best thing, I decided, was to make an announcement and request that all guests remain. There would be a few moans but they would stay. Anyone who had legitimate business elsewhere would have to be dealt with separately. Another thing I had to do soon was to inform Neville Gwynne of his wife's death and since he figured as a possible suspect I couldn't afford to have him clear out. But first of all I had to ring Lindon. The sooner I got a squad out here the better. It was now five-forty-five. Dinner on Sundays at Strathwood was at six-fifteen. If I made my announcement at the commencement of dinner I'd just have time to make my telephone calls and talk to Neville Gwynne.

We reached the office.

'Alec,' I said, 'I'd like to borrow your office for a while. I am going to call Inspector Lindon and then Headquarters and after that I want to talk to Neville Gwynne. One other thing. It will be an hour or more before the Headquarters team can get here and in the meantime I don't want anyone to leave. What I propose to do is to make an announcement at dinner and ask the guests to stay on until they have been interviewed. If by any chance somebody wants to leave before then, let me know and I'll talk to them.'

'It's very unlikely. Anyone who wanted to leave before dinner would have gone by now.' He paused and looked seriously at me. 'I suppose everyone comes under suspicion?'

I nodded.

'For the moment. All the males at any rate. Possibly the females too. I know it doesn't look like a woman's crime but Isobel wasn't very big and didn't strike me as being particularly strong so a determined woman could have murdered her. I could even be a suspect myself, that's why I may be taken off the case. There can't be any question of alibis until I know just when Isobel died so everyone's in the same boat.'

'I think you're safe enough. Judging by Pat's attitude towards you I very much doubt whether you've been alone for long this week-end.'

'That's true, but it's not an unmixed blessing. Depends. At any rate one consolation is that I can give Pat an alibi too though I hope to God I don't have to.'

'This thing's going to be a damned nuisance to everybody, in more ways than one,' said Alec feelingly. 'I suppose you'd like to make your calls in private?'

'I think I'd better.'

'All right. I'll leave you to it then.'

As soon as Alec had gone I sat down, reached for the phone on Alec's desk and rang Inspector Lindon. Because it was Sunday afternoon he was inclined to be testy about being disturbed but he changed his attitude when I explained in detail what had happened.

'My God, we certainly strike some funny ones,' he said. 'This is the first time I've ever known a detective to be on the spot when a murder has been committed. You should be able to work this one out, knowing all the people concerned.'

'I'm not so sure about that, it's more complicated than it sounds. And on that point I think you'd better bring another sergeant with you.'

'Why, Doug?'

'Well, I'm involved with these people. I could even be a suspect myself.'

'What bloody nonsense. You know the crowd so we're going to need you. I'm not tossing in an advantage like that just because you've developed some damned silly scruples. You're a cop, my lad, and it's time you learned that cops can't afford to have scruples. Leave it to me. I'll clear it with the Superintendent.'

'Will you ring Headquarters then?'

'Yes. I'll get things moving this end. You concentrate on keeping that mob there. I'll get a patrol car to give you a hand; there should be one in your area somewhere.'

'All right, Bob. One thing though. You'd better try and bring Dr Raines with you. We can't do a great deal until we know the time of death.'

'O.K. And there's one thing you can do for me. Get together a list of all the guests and the staff so that I'll know who's who. You might add a few notes if you have the time.'

'I'll do that. See you later.'

I replaced the receiver and looked at my watch. It was five to six. I'd have time for a quick word with Pat before talking to Neville Gwynne. I left the office and strolled casually across to the annexe, wondering what effect my announcement was going to have on the guests. The news was going to create a hell of a stir, that was certain. Pat opened her door as soon as I knocked. She looked anxious.

'What's happening, Douglas? Have you found out anything?'

I couldn't help a brief smile even though the situation wasn't a happy one for anybody.

'I'm not a miracle worker. It will probably be a long time before we find Isobel's murderer. It's going to be a very unpleasant process, not least for me. At the moment there's very little I can do but a team from Headquarters will be here in about an hour and a half.'

'How did she die, Douglas?'

I hesitated.

'It's very nasty.'

'Tell me. I'll have to know sooner or later.'

'She was hanged from one of the rafters in the store shed.'

'Oh God. The poor devil.'

'I'm afraid someone hated her very much indeed. It couldn't have been an easy death.'

'Does Neville know?'

'Not yet. I'm going to tell him in a few minutes.'

'Is there any chance that he . . .?'

'It's much too early to think about who killed her. It could have been anyone . . . any man at any rate. Even me.'

'You? How could you? You've been with me.'

'That's the only bright spot in the business from my point of view. I thought I might be taken off the case in view of the fact that I've been staying here but Inspector Lindon refuses to consider such an idea. Actually, I suppose it makes very little difference. I would have been required to stay here and help even if I wasn't part of the investigation team. As it is now I'll have to question people as if they were suspects, people like Alec and Peter Randall. In a way I wish I had been taken off the case.'

'Can't you resign or something?'

'Of course not. I'm only a sergeant. If the Inspector tells me to carry on I carry on and that's the end of it. However, it's probably better to be an active detective than what might appear to be a sort of police spy.'

'You're talking nonsense, Douglas. Everybody here likes you.'

I grinned wryly.

'As Douglas Gray, yes. But they may not be quite so happy with Detective Sergeant Gray. You'll see when I talk to them.'

'Talk to them?'

'I'm going to make an announcement just before dinner. I can't afford to have people leaving so I'll have to ask them to stay until our people get here.'

'Are you going to tell them why?'

'Naturally. I can't ask them to hang around without giving them a very good reason. As it is some of them are going to be a bit upset. Obviously most of them will have nothing to contribute and many of them will have alibis but I can't make any exceptions, certainly not until I know when Isobel died.'

'I see what you mean about not being so popular. Dinner's going to be a bit of an ordeal, isn't it?'

'I've been thinking about that. Once I've made my announcement I want to get out of the dining-room fast, I don't want to be baled up with a lot of questions and requests for preferential treatment. I'll get Alec to arrange a tray for me . . . and for you too, otherwise you'll be pestered to death.'

'That's a good idea. We can eat here.'

'Well, I'd better be off. I'll be back in time for dinner. You may have the pleasure of getting a drink ready, a good strong whisky, I think.'

I left Pat and hurried over to the main house looking for Alec. I found him in the hall.

'I'm going to talk to Gwynne now,' I told him. 'Is he still in his cabin?'

'As far as I know. He hasn't left Strathwood at any rate.'

'He seems to be taking Isobel's disappearance pretty calmly.'

'I don't know. He's been drinking a bit. I think he still hopes she'll turn up.'

'This is going to knock him for a six . . . unless he murdered her.'

'Could he have done that, Douglas?'

'God knows. It's much too soon to even think about it.

All the same I have to regard him as a possible suspect, at least until I know more about when Isobel died and can confirm that he wasn't here when her death occurred. For the moment I think I'll just tell him that his wife's body has been found and leave it at that.'

'Would you like me to come with you?'

I thought it over for a few seconds and began to see considerable merit in Alec's suggestion. Although I hadn't said so to Alec I knew that Neville Gwynne was going to become a prime suspect in the eyes of Inspector Lindon merely because he was Isobel's husband and could have had a strong motive. At this point I didn't want to question him and perhaps scare him into doing something desperate like clearing out, so Alec's presence might make it easier for me to talk to him as a fellow guest rather than an investigating detective. In short, I was anxious to maintain a *status quo* until our doctor had examined the body and we had some sound basis to work on.

'I think that would be a good idea,' I said to Alec. 'It's a very unpleasant business telling a man that his wife has been murdered, particularly in this case when the thing was done so brutally. Your presence may help to calm him down.'

Gwynne's cabin was one of half a dozen small cottages built amongst the trees well behind the main building. Each of them contained a bedroom-living-room with a couple of divan beds, comfortable furniture and a tiny bathroom. Alec knocked at the half-open door and we stepped inside. I was a little shocked at Gwynne's appearance. I knew he was supposed to be something of a weakling where Isobel was concerned but nothing of this had shown in his normal appearance, which to my eyes had been that of a fairly successful business man, well-dressed, capable and self-confident. Now he looked pale, dishevelled and careworn. A bottle of whisky and a tumbler were on the low table beside him and he had obviously been drinking but as he looked up at us he seemed in full command of his faculties. I stood back and allowed Alec to speak first.

'Neville,' he said. 'We have some bad news for you. You had better prepare yourself for a shock.'

Gwynne looked first at Alec and then at me. He seemed worried and anxious but not nervous. I didn't think he grasped the idea that what we were about to tell him was really serious but thought that we were using conventional terms to describe something unpleasant but not vital. He knew it referred to Isobel though.

'What is it?' he said. 'Isobel?'

Alec answered.

'She's dead, Neville.'

He appeared not to take it in for a moment. Then he sagged.

'Dead?' he said, almost whispering. 'Where?'

'Look, better take a drink, Neville. I'll pour it for you.'

Alec tipped some whisky into a glass and gave it to Neville. Neville sipped it neat. He recovered a little.

'This is a hell of a shock. What happened? Where is she?'

'Take it easy, Neville. She's here, on the property. But she didn't die naturally. Somebody killed her.'

Neville started to rise.

'Killed her? Who did?'

Alec pushed him back in his chair.

'Just relax. There's nothing you can do. I've brought Detective Sergeant Gray along. He'll do what he can.'

Gwynne looked up quickly.

'Detective?' he said to me. 'I thought you were a friend of Pat Morland's.'

'I am. I've been a friend of hers for years. It's just coincidence that I happen to be a detective too.'

'It's certain that she was . . . that somebody killed her?'

'I'm afraid so, but try not to think about it. A police squad will be here before long and we'll do our best to find out who killed your wife. In the meantime I suggest you stay here quietly.'

'Can I see her?'

'It would be better if you didn't. Perhaps later, if you feel up to it.'

Gwynne put his glass down. He had drunk very little whisky and that, I thought, was a good sign.

'When did it happen?' he asked. 'While I was away?'

'We don't know yet. Is there anyone you'd like to talk to?'

'Not now. I think I'll take an aspirin or something. Will the police want to talk to me?'

'Later. Just rest if you can. Have you got an aspirin?'

'Yes. There are some here.'

'Well take a couple and lie down. I'll come back when we've sorted things out a bit.'

Gwynne nodded despondently. I left with Alec.

'I think he took it very well,' Alec said when we were outside.

'He's a queer bird, sitting there all by himself. You'd think he'd want to talk to somebody. However, I don't think he'll run away.'

We went back to the office and I arranged with Alec to send over a couple of trays for Pat and me. He agreed and suggested he send some food over to Gwynne.

'Good idea,' I said. 'It might help to take his mind off things. Now I think I'd better go and talk to the guests. You'd better come with me, Alec, and introduce me as a policeman; that might soften the shock a bit.'

Alec and I walked into the dining-room. It was now well after six-fifteen and everyone appeared to be present, except of course Pat and Neville Gwynne. We took up a position near the door and Alec rapped sharply on the wall behind him and spoke in a firm voice.

'May I have your attention, please.'

It took a few seconds for animated conversations to die down and then there was silence, even the waitresses pausing in their work.

'I'm afraid I have some very serious news for you,' Alec said and then paused. 'Mrs Gwynne has been found but I regret to say that she is dead. I am now going to ask Detective Sergeant Gray of the C.I.B. to amplify my statement a little. As you know, Sergeant Gray was a guest here but in the circumstances he has been obliged to resume his official status as a member of the C.I.B. Thank you. Sergeant Gray.'

I stepped forward and waited for the buzz of conversation to cease. Then I spoke in my most official voice.

'I won't keep you a moment. I just want to say that Mrs Gwynne's body has been found in circumstances that make a police investigation necessary. Within an hour from now a team from C.I.B. Headquarters, led by a Detective Inspector, will be here and I must ask you not to leave Strathwood until it arrives. You will understand that everyone here will have to be interviewed and a great many questions asked and I hope that you will give the police your active co-operation in the difficult task of finding Mrs Gwynne's murderer. Thank you.'

My use of the term murderer was calculated and deliberate; I hoped it would stifle any special pleas to leave before the police team arrived. Alec and I left as a spate of talk began as I was anxious to avoid being questioned. We stepped into the hall just as a patrol car arrived at the front door and I sent it back to the entrance of the main drive with instructions to stop anyone from leaving. If anyone tried to I was to be informed at once. I was aware of course that if a murderer was included amongst the guests at Strathwood and he desperately wanted to escape he could do so whenever he wished, on foot. But it would have taken an army to cover every possible exit and had he wanted to escape he would have done so long before this. My guess was that the murderer thought he was safe and was going to brazen it out.

Before I left the main building for a belated dinner with Pat I asked Alec whether he could provide me with a complete list of guests and their addresses and the names of his staff. He said he'd have it ready by the time I'd finished dinner and I rushed off to the annexe.

Pat had a whisky waiting for me, which I needed. One didn't often enjoy the luxury of a drink on the job but this time I thought I'd earned it. My anomalous position as half guest, half policeman made my job a difficult one.

I hurried through dinner, eaten awkwardly with a tray on my knees while sitting on the edge of the bed, and left Pat to return the trays to the kitchen while I went back to the office. I was busy adding a few notes to the guest list when the cavalcade from Headquarters arrived. Inspector Lindon lumbered in, surprisingly cheerful seeing that he had been dragged out on a Sunday night. I introduced him to Alec Reeves and then asked him whether he had brought Dr Raines with him. He said he had so I suggested that the first thing to do was to view the body. He agreed.

I led the way out of the office on to the drive where we were joined by Dr Raines, the police surgeon; a photographer; a fingerprint man and a couple of constables. Watched by a few inquisitive guests from the windows of the lounge we trailed along the main drive, turned right up the path leading to the cabins, passed the yard at the end of the stables and came to a halt outside the store shed. I took the key from my pocket and unlocked the door and then used a handkerchief to turn the brass handle.

'Anything likely to be on that?' asked Lindon.

'I doubt it. At least two people have handled it since the murder but it might be worth while checking it. There's a faint chance that the murderer left his prints.'

I opened the door, and because it was now getting dark, felt for the switch and turned on the light, a single unshaded bulb of low power hanging a little above and in front of the body. I moved back to allow the Inspector to enter.

'Christ!' Lindon said, stopping so suddenly that Raines cannoned into the Inspector's huge bulk.

The doctor moved round and stared with Lindon at Isobel's nude body. The dull light from the weak lamp gave the scene something of the appearance of an early Dutch still life only instead of a hanging pheasant there was a pale, naked female form.

Raines moved forward.

'My God, somebody certainly hated that girl,' he said softly.

We were silent for a moment or two.

'The first thing we want to know is when she died,' I said. 'It's very important, Doc.'

'It always is. But I can't do much until you've cut her down and then I'll need a better light than this. But I'll take a quick look now if you like.'

Raines went over to the body and began to feel the limbs, dispassionately, as if the flesh was no longer human.

'See if you can organize a better light, Doug,' Lindon said to me.

I went to the office and found Alec. He told me he had a car inspection lamp.'

'Has it got a long lead?'

'Oh yes. We use it to work on the tractor. There's a good thirty feet of it. But you'll have to plug it in in the other half of the store shed.'

Alec found the lamp and came back with me to open the locked section of the store shed. I plugged the lamp in and carried it into where the body was. The photographer was just taking his last shots and I waited until he had finished before hanging the inspection lamp on a convenient nail and switching it on.

'Dr Raines says she died some time during the early hours of Sunday morning,' Lindon said to me.

'It's a rough guess, a very rough one,' said Raines, not flippant for once. 'Between maybe twelve and three. But I'll give you a better estimate when I've had a proper look at her.'

'It couldn't have been earlier?' I asked Raines.

'Well how much earlier?'

'Early on Saturday evening?'

'Not a chance, Doug. Mind you I'm not laying bets at this stage but she's still as stiff as a board and I very much doubt whether she died any earlier than midnight and the chances are that it was quite a lot later.'

'It was dark then,' I said to Lindon thoughtfully. 'I wonder how he managed? I can't imagine him switching on the light.'

Lindon looked around the crowded shed.

'He must have been very familiar with the place. Or perhaps he used a torch.'

'A torch could have attracted attention.'

'Would it? At one o'clock in the morning?'

'A lot depends on just when she was murdered. After about one-fifteen when most of the people here had gone to bed there wouldn't have been anyone around here and he may have been able to use a torch providing he was careful.'

'He would have had his hands full tying her up, not to mention putting that gag on her, with one hand holding a torch. But perhaps he rested it on the floor.'

'Actually there's a lamp on the car park outside. It would have sent sufficient light through the window for someone who knew his way around in here. But I don't think it's left on all night. We'll have to ask Alec Reeves.'

'Looks as if it might have been a pre-arranged job in one way. If the murderer had got everything ready beforehand he wouldn't have needed a great deal of light. On the other hand the indications are that he did this in a blinding rage, not as the result of careful planning.'

I wasn't so sure.

'If he fixed up everything first the job would have been a hell of a lot easier. Hunting around for bits of string in the semi-darkness would have been difficult . . . and slow.'

I had, of course, thought of the possibility that Gwynne had murdered his wife before setting off for town on Saturday night but, assuming that he did in fact go to town, the medical evidence made it impossible. Dr Raines was usually reliable in such matters and I doubted that there would be much change from his first estimate.

'We'd better get her down now,' said Inspector Lindon. 'Doug, do you think you can organize a bench of some kind?'

'I think so. There's enough material right here.'

I grabbed some of the planks from against the wall and with the help of a constable made a rough bier by using a couple of boxes as supports. It was a bit low but Raines wasn't very tall and he could manage. Lindon unhooked the inspection lamp and took a look at the leather strap.

'I can't see that the knots are going to help us much,' he said. 'Obviously they weren't tied by a boy scout or a deep-sea sailor. Anyway we'll cut through the middle and keep the top end intact. Who's got a penknife?'

'Here, use this,' said Raines.

Lindon hesitated.

'It's all right,' Raines said. 'It's an old blade. I can put a new one in if I find it necessary to use it.'

Lindon took the scalpel and immediately handed it to me.

'You're younger than I am, Doug, you can do the cutting. You'll have to stand on that box.'

'Not that one. The murderer used it and it may have something useful on it.'

Using my handkerchief again I moved both the box and the chair, putting them on one side for transport to Headquarters later. I found a suitable crate and placed it in position by the body.

'Let's get organized,' said Lindon. 'You two can take the weight while Doug cuts the strap, but handle her carefully.'

The two constables moved over to the body, somewhat gingerly. I climbed up on the crate. Lindon directed operations.

'Right. Take the weight now. Carefully does it. Got her?'

There wasn't much room to manoeuvre but the two men took a grip of the lower part of the body and I leaned forward on my slightly wobbly crate.

'We've got her,' said one of the constables.

'Good. You can cut now, Doug.'

I cut the strap. The constables, not looking very happy, carried the body over to the improvised bier and delicately laid it down. It rested grotesquely on the bound wrists.

'Will somebody shove that light back?' asked Raines. 'Where it was before will do.'

I moved the lamp and hung it on the wall so that it threw a brilliant light over the discoloured body. Raines started to move the clothes that were now tangled around the ankles and quickly found that Isobel's ankles were bound with twine. I collected the dress and other garments as Raines took some small scissors and began to cut through the twine which had embedded itself and pressed the nylon deeply into the flesh. He cut well away from the knots and detached the twine slowly, using the delicate care of the surgeon. With Lindon's help he turned the body over and repeated the treatment at the wrists.

As Raines released the strap from around the neck and

56

then started to work on the gag he looked up at Lindon.

'Why don't you two go outside for a while?' he said. 'She's not going to be a very pleasant sight and I don't particularly want you breathing down my neck.'

'All right, Doc, we'll leave you to it.'

'I won't be very long. There's not much I can do here. The ambulance will be along in a few minutes and unless there is any special reason for keeping her here I'll take her away.'

'As far as I'm concerned you can take her, Doc. What about you, Doug?'

'I'm mostly interested in knowing the time she died, but there are one or two other things. Are there any marks on the body? Signs of a struggle? Bruises?'

'I haven't noticed any so far but if I find anything I'll let you know. What else?'

'She did die of strangulation?'

'There's no doubt about that.'

'She wasn't dead when she was strung up then?'

'Oh no. She died here, on the spot.'

'One other thing then.' I turned to Lindon. 'Her husband's here. He wants to see her. We could get his identification at the same time.'

'Good idea. That all right with you, Doc?'

'Yes. I'll tell you what. Wait till the ambulance gets here, it shouldn't be long, and I'll get her on to a stretcher and covered up. The poor bastard's not going to enjoy seeing her as she is so I'll get her straightened up a bit.'

Lindon and I went outside. The two constables had anticipated us and were having a quiet chat in the darkness. The Inspector told one of them to stay put.

'Dr Raines is still inside. I want you to keep an eye open for the ambulance and when it comes let me know. I'll be over in the main building.' He turned to the second constable. 'Bill, you can wander down to the main gate and tell the ambulance where to go. You can tell that patrol car crew we've finished with them and then come back to the house and stand by.'

Lindon and I started to walk slowly down towards the house.

'This husband,' he said. 'Could he have killed his wife?'

'Not if his story is true. I haven't actually questioned him but he was supposed to be in Sydney last night. Of course he could have come back during the night.'

As soon as we reached the office I asked Alec whether we could take it over for a while or whether he had some other room we could use.

'I suppose you are going to question everybody?' he asked.

'We'll have to, Alec.'

'Will you let the guests go when you have finished with them?'

The Inspector answered.

'Those we are satisfied had nothing to do with the murder of Mrs Gwynne.'

Alec shrugged helplessly.

'I have no objection to you using this office but all my papers, money, receipt books and records are in here. The guests will want to pay their bills.' He smiled thinly. 'At least, I hope they will. How about a corner of the dining-room?'

'That will do,' said Lindon. 'All we need is a table and a couple of chairs . . . no, three chairs.'

Alec smiled.

'There's no shortage of chairs in the dining-room and I'll see that you are not disturbed.'

I gathered my notes together and Lindon and I went to the dining-room and settled down at a table near the door.

'Have you got a list of the guests?' Lindon asked me.

'Yes, but I haven't had time to add many notes.'

'That's all right. You'd better give me the story in a bit

more detail than you did over the phone. Then we'll get Gwynne over. Is he being guarded by the way?'

'No. I don't think he should be either. If he's guilty he'd be crazy to run away at this stage.'

'Hmm. I guess you're right. Well, let's have it. And give me that list so I can memorize the names.'

It didn't take long to give the Inspector a fairly detailed account of all that had happened during the week-end. He listened in silence and I knew he'd remember it all. Long experience had given him the faculty of quickly grasping the mechanics of a situation; who did what and when were meat and drink to him.

'It looks as if Mrs Gwynne was killed some time after the party,' said Lindon thoughtfully. 'But she wasn't at the party and the two men she'd had most to deal with weren't there either. That's a bit odd, isn't it?'

'It looks a bit odd, I agree, but it's a bit early to come to any conclusions. As I said, Scott left to go back to Sydney straight after dinner last night. Fuller was here this morning but I haven't seen him around since then so he may have cleared out too.'

'So Scott left at about the same time as Neville Gwynne?'

'Apparently. But I haven't questioned anybody yet so I don't know the precise timing.'

'Well let's make a start with Gwynne, then we'll deal with the rest one at a time. Will you get him, Doug?'

I nodded and left the dining-room but I didn't go straight to Gwynne's cabin. I was anxious to have a word with Pat so I hurried to the annexe. I found Pat waiting anxiously in her room. I spoke quickly.

'I haven't much time, Pat, but I thought I'd better warn you. You will have to be questioned like everyone else but the only point that really concerns you is where you were when Isobel died.'

'When was that, Douglas?'

'It's a bit awkward. In fact it could be very embarrassing for you. Isobel died during the night, probably about one in the morning or later. We won't know precisely for a while but if it was after one o'clock . . .'

'Oh Lord,' said Pat. 'You know quite well where I was after one o'clock but do I have to tell the Inspector?'

'I don't think you'll be able to get out of it, Pat, but I'll break the ice first. I'll just have to tell Lindon that we were together but I'll try and avoid telling him that we were in bed. Probably he'll be satisfied with that.'

'Listen, Douglas, I don't mind admitting that I slept with you last night if it's necessary. But how will I know whether it's necessary? What do I say if you're not there when the Inspector talks to me?'

'I'll almost certainly be there but if by any chance I'm not, just say that you were with me. Uncle Bob won't press you after I've talked to him.'

'Goodness. I hope not.' She smiled at me. 'This is what I get for misbehaving with a policeman.'

'It was worth it, wasn't it?'

She just smiled and I kissed her quickly.

'If I were you I'd join the crowd in the house now. It's terribly dull sitting around here on your own. But if anyone asks you questions, you know nothing. Particularly, don't say a word about when Isobel died.'

I smiled at her and made for Gwynne's cabin at a fast walk. To my surprise he was sitting in his chair calmly reading. He looked up and threw the book aside rather shamefacedly as I entered the cottage after a rapid knock.

'I had to do something,' he explained. 'Is there any news?'

'Nothing yet but I want you to come with me and talk to Inspector Lindon.'

'Lindon? What's he like?'

'Oh, big, solid, easygoing. Pleasant to talk to.'

Gwynne stood up. He looked a little nervous but was well in control of himself. We went over to the dining-room, watched by curious eyes as we passed the open door of the lounge. I introduced Gwynne to the Inspector who at once invited Gwynne to sit down and told me to offer Gwynne a cigarette. Lindon smoked nothing but a pipe, thus saving himself quite a lot of money at my expense. The atmosphere was casual by design.

'I understand you spend quite a lot of time here,' said Lindon amiably, digging into his pocket for his pipe. You come here most week-ends?'

'We . . . we liked the place.'

'Yes. It looks very pleasant. Now I've been told that you had to break your week-end. You left here just after dinner last night to go to Mascot. Is that right?'

'Yes.'

'When was this arranged?'

Gwynne answered in a firm voice.

'Last week. I wanted to cancel our week-end here as it was to be interrupted but Isobel wouldn't hear of it. So we came up.'

'Why did you have to go to Mascot, Mr Gwynne?'

'I'm in the advertising business. The impression I make on clients is all-important. This was a special client of mine or I wouldn't have bothered to go all the way to Mascot to pick him up and take him to his hotel. Anyway I did so and then entertained him for the evening.'

Lindon leaned back and lit his pipe. He spoke to Gwynne through a cloud of blue smoke.

'Your wife didn't go with you?'

'No. She wouldn't.'

'Had you expected her to?'

'Not really. I just hoped she would on this occasion.'

'Did she give any reason for refusing?'

'She didn't like my clients. She said they were a lot of dull, old men. She wanted to stay for the party.'

'Did she say that specifically?'

'Oh yes. She loved parties.'

'But she wasn't at the party. Can you give us any reason for her not going?'

'I just don't understand it.'

'Mr Gwynne. Your wife died very late on Saturday night, or perhaps I should say early on Sunday morning. We are anxious to know where she was during the early part of the evening. Can you help us?'

Gwynne didn't say anything at first. Then he took a deep breath.

'Inspector,' he said, 'my wife was what one might call gay. She was fond of dancing and parties and was very attractive to men. But it was all fun to her and she wouldn't have allowed any man to go too far with her. When I heard that she had apparently gone away from here I didn't know what to think, but that Scott fellow had been hanging around her a good deal and the only conclusion I could come to was that he had talked her into going away with him. I didn't believe she would do such a thing but there just didn't seem to be any other explanation.'

I'm afraid I stared at Gwynne rather and even Lindon was frowning as if puzzled. The ideas Gwynne had just put forth were so diametrically opposed to the description I'd given the Inspector that I could have been talking about a totally different person. I didn't understand how an intelligent man could be so easily deceived. Isobel had been attractive up to a point but what she offered was sex and she offered it in the challenging sort of way that would tempt a man whose mind was already turned in that direction but would offend or irritate others.

Lindon shook his head slightly as if to clear the doubt from his mind and started on a new tack.

'Now will you please tell us exactly what you did on Saturday night?'

'Certainly. I picked up my client at Mascot . . .'

62

'His name, please.'

'John Archer of Archer Fabrications Limited. You've heard of them of course.'

'Yes. Where did you take him?'

'To the Wentworth Hotel. I'd already booked a suite for him there.'

'I see. What did you do then?'

'We had a couple of drinks in his suite and then I took him to the Silver Spade. We stayed there until about one and then went back to the Wentworth. We had a nightcap and then I said good night to him and went to my flat.'

'Why didn't you return to Strathwood?'

'I considered it a little too late to drive all that way.'

'What time did you leave the Wentworth then?'

'About half past one.'

Lindon looked down at the list of guests I had given him earlier.

'You live at Point Piper, I see.'

'Yes.'

'I suppose no one saw you enter your flat by any chance?'

'Well, not exactly. But the taxi-driver saw me as far as the building.'

'*Taxi-driver?*' Lindon looked puzzled. 'Weren't you driving your own car?'

'No. I knew I was going to have a fair bit to drink one way and another so what with these breathalyser tests I decided it would be safer to put my car in the Wentworth car park and leave it there overnight. I took Archer to the Silver Spade and back by taxi and then got another one home later. This morning I took a taxi from my flat to the Wentworth, picked up my car and drove out here.'

'Would you remember the names of any of these taxis?'

'Oh yes. The R.S.L. Cab Company. I always use them. I have an account there.'

'In that case they'd have a record of these trips of yours?'

'Of course. I use taxis a lot in my business.' He smiled faintly. 'Taxi fares go on my expense account so I rarely pay cash.'

It looked as if Gwynne had an absolutely cast-iron alibi. Of course, after dismissing his R.S.L. cab he could have taken some unknown cab back to the Wentworth to pick up his car but even his Jaguar couldn't have got him to Strathwood before about half past three and by that time, unless Dr Raines' estimate was wildly inaccurate, his wife was dead. The Wentworth car park would no doubt have a record if he had taken his car away during the night and returned it later so there was no chance that he had murdered his wife. Besides, where had she been between the time he left her on the Strathwood car park and the time she died?

'Can you tell us exactly what time you left here last night?'

'Not to the minute but it must have been about ten to seven, I imagine. I know I was running a little late.'

'When you drove off you actually left your wife standing on the car park?'

'Yes. We had a last-minute argument but she refused to come with me. I must confess I was a bit annoyed at her unreasonable attitude but I had no time to waste so I drove off and left her there.'

'Was there anyone else on the car park or anywhere near it when you left?'

'I didn't see anyone.'

The Inspector frowned down at the table for several seconds and then looked up at Gwynne. His voice was quiet.

'Mr Gwynne,' he said, 'I am going to ask you what you may think is a very distasteful question. But somebody murdered your wife and whoever it was must have had a very powerful motive. Are you being quite honest when you say that your wife wouldn't have allowed a man to go too far with her? In other words, to your knowledge could she have had an affair with a man that might have provoked a situation leading to her murder?'

Gwynne looked grim and then suddenly appealing.

'Look, Inspector, I realize that one can't always know another person well enough to be certain about everything they do and I admit that my wife was what one might call flirtatious. She liked men. But I'm sure she wouldn't have gone as far as sleeping with another man. She wasn't even particularly fond of sex and I should know.'

I could see that Lindon had great difficulty in squaring what Gwynne had just said with what I had told him about Isobel Gwynne. In fact if Alec Reeves hadn't told me about his encounter with her I might have believed that her sexual activities had been grossly exaggerated. But the murder itself had strongly sexual overtones, the furious ripping of her clothes was some kind of symbolic act. Her dress had been torn apart from neckline to hem in one vicious wrench. I felt tempted to put this to Gwynne but it was a distressing question so I left it to Lindon to discuss it if he wished. He didn't though. He told Gwynne he had no more questions to ask for the moment and did he feel up to identifying the body as that of his wife.

'It's a formality, Mr Gwynne, but it's usual to ask a relative or someone close to the deceased to make a formal identification. We'll do what we can to make it as easy as possible for you.'

Gwynne's face registered acute dislike but he consented, if rather reluctantly. Lindon sent me over to the store shed to see that all was in readiness. Raines had finished his work and the body was now set up on a stretcher and completely covered. The ambulance was waiting on the drive.

'I couldn't do very much, Doug,' Raines said to me. 'She's still not a pleasant sight. It might be an idea to give the poor bastard a stiff drink first.'

'All right, Doc. I'll bring him over shortly. Any change

65

in the time of death?'

'Not much. It isn't easy to be precise in cases like this. The best I can do is between twelve-thirty and two-thirty.'

'Thanks, Doc. I'll get Gwynne.'

I went back to the dining-room and told Gwynne that it might be an idea if he had a good stiff drink. He refused.

'I'll need it later,' he said, obviously steeling himself for his ordeal.

Lindon and I took him over to the store shed. Raines met us and took charge. I followed the two of them into the shed and stood just behind Gwynne in case he collapsed. Raines gently uncovered Isobel's distorted face, Gwynne looked quickly and at once turned away. I took his arm.

'It's her,' he said. 'Let me go. I must get outside.'

We went outside. Gwynne leant up against the wall of the shed for a few seconds and then straightened up.

'Sorry,' he said. 'It was a terrible shock. What did they do to her?'

'Don't think about it,' said the Inspector. 'It's over now. Sergeant, take Mr Gwynne back to the house and see if you can organize a brandy.'

I moved off with Gwynne.

'She was strangled, wasn't she?' he asked.

'It was over very quickly,' I said, wondering if even Gwynne would believe the lie.

We reached the house and Alec produced some brandy. Gwynne drank some quickly and then said he felt all right.

'Do you think you are fit to drive?' I asked him. 'I can detail a man to drive you if you don't feel up to it.'

'No. I'll be all right. I'd sooner be on my own.'

I took him to his cabin and helped him pack his bag.

'I suppose I'd better leave her things?' he said to me.

'For the moment. Just grab your stuff together and get home. If I were you I'd give myself another drink and hop into bed.'

'I'll do that. Thanks.'

I saw him to his car and watched him drive away. The ambulance had already gone, its lights were just turning out of the drive. Gwynne, I noted, drove slowly and carefully. He would be all right. I went back to Lindon. He was talking to Dr Raines, who was about to depart. Raines was laying down the law.

'You take my tip and look for a homicidal maniac,' he said. 'Whoever murdered that girl was vicious. He didn't merely murder her, he punished her, a ritual hanging, just about. I'd say he was temporarily insane or at any rate in a hell of a temper. The way those clothes are torn shows that.'

'It's what our newspapers are going to call a sex murder, which is probably true. There must have been some sexual jealousy or something like that behind it. By the way, Doc, will you check whether she had sexual intercourse just before she died?'

'I'll do that. Have you any particular reason for thinking she may have?'

'Well yes. Apparently she was a bit of a nympho and as far as we can make out she was missing from about seven until the body was found this afternoon. We suspect that she might have been with some man, possibly the one who killed her.'

'All right. Anything else?'

'Nothing in particular. Let us know if you find anything unusual though.'

'You can rest assured on that point. I'll let you have a report as soon as I can.'

We saw Dr Raines off and walked back to the house.

'I think we might talk to Alec Reeves next,' I suggested to Lindon. 'He can fill in on anything you want to know about the set-up here.'

It crossed my mind that I ought to warn the Inspector

that Reeves could be considered a possible suspect in view of what he had told me. But I thought it best to let Lindon get the general picture before volunteering specific evidence. Lindon would no doubt think of every man in the place as a potential murderer until he learned otherwise. On that score I had some explaining to do myself, but that could wait.

Once in the house we called Alec into the dining-room and once more my cigarettes came in useful as a means of setting a casual tone to the investigation. As Alec sat down, Lindon leaned back as comfortably as he could in a hard dining-room chair and began to fill his pipe, an action that made him look rather like a benevolent uncle. This was the reason why he was known to the younger members of the detective force as Uncle Bob though the nickname wasn't used in his hearing.

'I think we'd better start with this party last night, Mr Reeves,' he said amiably. 'I take it that it was a regular Saturday night affair?'

'Well, more or less. It's not an organized entertainment, just something the guests do on their own initiative.'

'And Mrs Gwynne would normally have been present?'

'Yes, when the Gwynnes were here, of course.'

'So when she didn't appear you assumed that she'd gone with her husband?'

'Naturally.'

'You didn't consider the possibility that she might have gone elsewhere?'

'Not for a moment. She was very fond of parties and had she not gone with her husband she would have been here, I am certain.'

'I see. Now when did this party end?'

Alec reflected for a moment.

'It didn't end suddenly, you know. Some people started to drift off to bed soon after midnight but I suppose it was close to one o'clock when it finally packed up. I always take a look round last thing, just to make sure no one has left a cigarette burning and that sort of thing and I think it was about one when I went to my room.'

'Did you go straight to bed?'

Alec took a quick glance at me. He was evidently recalling the story he had told Pat and me about Isobel's visit to him. As a matter of fact I was thinking about that myself. He hadn't admitted having had anything further to do with her but for all I knew he had been carrying on a torrid affair with her for months. Isobel had not been the sort of woman to be content with one casual night's entertainment and Alec was ideally placed to receive her favours. This was one of the awkward situations arising out of knowing the people concerned in the case. I didn't for one moment believe that Alec had murdered Isobel yet I had to admit the possibility existed. He knew all about the store shed, of course, and was in a position to plan Isobel's death in advance. She may have become a nuisance to him or given some other reason for getting rid of her. I certainly did not know him well enough to be certain whether he was capable of murder or not. He had a dark, rather saturnine countenance that could have concealed very deep emotions.

'Oh yes,' he said. 'I went to bed almost immediately.'

Lindon didn't notice Alec's slight delay in answering.

'Where is your room, Mr Reeves?'

'Right next to the office.'

'Did you hear anything suspicious during the night? People leaving the building, for example?'

Alec smiled a little.

'No, but if I had I wouldn't have regarded it as suspicious. The guests are all adults and if they want to wander about during the night that's their business.'

'Do they?' the Inspector asked suspiciously.

'Sometimes. It has been known for people to go for

moonlight rides in the small hours but in that case I have to know. I don't allow guests to take horses out at night unless they are experienced and competent riders.'

Lindon grunted. Moonlight riding was something entirely beyond his experience.

'Was it common knowledge among your guests that Mr Gwynne was going to Sydney on Saturday night?'

'I think so. He told me when they first arrived and I understand that he and his wife were arguing publicly during dinner about whether she should go with him or not.'

'Hmm. There's something very puzzling about this. We are satisfied that Mrs Gwynne didn't go to Sydney with her husband. Are you sure you have no idea where she could have been between the time Mr Gwynne left and the time she was murdered?'

'I don't know when that was.'

'Ah. Of course not. Well as far as we can determine at the moment she died somewhere round one o'clock or a bit later. In other words she was here, somewhere in the area, for several hours. Could she have been with another guest for instance?'

'Inspector. As far as I know she wasn't seen after she left the house to see her husband off. She could have been somewhere here I suppose or she could have gone off somewhere else and come back later. But I don't follow my guests around so I have no idea where she could have been or with whom.'

It was clear that if Alec had any suspicions he wasn't going to voice them. I intervened with a question.

'Are all the cabins occupied, Alec?' I asked. 'Aren't some of them empty?'

'Four are occupied and three are empty.'

'Are the empty ones locked?'

'They are. But it wouldn't be all that difficult to get into one of them.'

70

'What are you suggesting, Doug?' Lindon asked. 'That she spent the evening with someone in one of the empty cabins?'

'Why should she do that?' asked Alec. 'She had a cabin of her own.'

'Alec,' I said. 'We are all aware of what kind of woman Isobel was. I'm suggesting that she may have spent the early part of the evening with some man, I haven't any idea who. But if she took him to her own cottage there was a risk that someone might have discovered her there. It's not certain that everyone believed she had gone to town and in any case if she was with a man she would want to be as safe from discovery as possible. One of the empty cottages would make a rather convenient love nest, don't you think?'

'I don't know. She would have had to break in.'

'Wasn't she the sort of person who would do just that?'

'I wouldn't put it past her but . . .' Alec shrugged. 'She could have used her own cabin. She would have been safe enough there with the light out.'

'We'll check on it,' said Lindon. 'Who was in the other cottages?'

'Three married couples. They're on your list. The Connells, the Dentons and the Harrows, if I remember correctly.'

'Well, they couldn't have seen her,' I said. 'They would have said so if they had.'

'Nobody saw her,' said Alec gloomily. 'Personally I think she went off with somebody and that somebody brought her back later and murdered her.'

'You may be right. By the way Rodney Fuller wasn't at the party last night but he was here this morning. I haven't seen him around this afternoon. Is he still here?'

'No. He left shortly after lunch.'

'Did he say why he was leaving so early?'

'No. As I told you, I don't ask questions. I assumed he

had an appointment in town.'

'You've no idea where he was last night?'

'None at all. But some of the people who come here regularly have made friends in the district. He may have gone visiting.'

'One last question, Alec. The light on the car park. Is it on all night?'

'No. I switch it off before I go to bed. There are lights on all night in the main house and the annexe but none outside.'

We let Alec go at this point as there didn't seem to be anything more he could tell us. Lindon lit his pipe, which had gone out. He added the match to a little criss-cross pile he'd made on a corner of the table.

'This is a funny sort of set-up,' he said to me pensively. 'I wonder where that girl got to?'

'The only thing I'm certain of is that she was with a man. But where, heaven only knows.'

'I'd like to know who the man was.'

'I don't doubt it,' I said. 'If we knew that, we'd probably know the murderer. But I think I'd better put you in the picture a bit more. As I told Dr Raines, Mrs Gwynne was something close to a nymphomaniac . . .'

'What the devil *is* a nymphomaniac? I know it's supposed to mean a woman who's a bit fond of sex but is it an illness or what?'

'I guess it is, in a way. It's a psychological state. I don't know whether Isobel Gwynne was technically a nymphomaniac but from all accounts she was very fond of men. Remember her husband admitted she was a bit flirtatious, as he called it, but according to Alec she was very much worse than that.'

'Alec?'

'Yes. He's the only man I *know* she slept with though I suspect that she did so with other men here.'

'What's this about Alec Reeves? How do you know she

72

slept with him?'

'Because he told me. She came to his room one night wearing nothing but a flimsy dressing-gown and wouldn't go away.'

'God Almighty! Where the devil was her husband?'

'He wasn't here that night.'

'You didn't tell me about this before, Doug.'

'I didn't want you to start off with any prejudices. Alec couldn't have been with Mrs Gwynne during the early part of the evening because he was at the party but he has no alibi for the time she died. You see she could have gone off with someone and returned some time after one. I don't know that Alec continued his association with the woman but it's the sort of thing that happens and he may have been waiting for her some time after one in a madly jealous mood. I've known Alec for some years but only very slightly so I can't say how he would react in that sort of situation but I'm damned sure he'd be a nasty man to cross if he was in a temper.'

The Inspector frowned at me across the table.

'It doesn't look so good, does it? He'd know about that store shed and what was in it. Who better?'

'True. But you can look at that both ways. Would he have killed her there? He'd surely realize that we'd suspect him just because he *was* familiar with the shed.'

'How often is it used?'

'Alec says fairly frequently. And there's some support for his claim in that the handyman went there this afternoon.'

'That might have been just bad luck. Reeves may know that it's so seldom visited the body could have stayed there for days. We might have had difficulty in establishing the time of death.'

'That's possible but Alec's not the only man here who was mixed up with Isobel. There was that character Scott who Neville Gwynne was so fussed about for a start.'

'Any truth in that?'

'I don't really know, Bob. It could be just idle gossip. The only real evidence I have about her activities comes from Alec's story but if she was willing to go as far as she did with him, I don't see why she shouldn't have done so with other men, including Scott.'

'We're relying rather a lot on what Reeves said. Was he telling the truth?'

'Why should he volunteer the information if it wasn't true? This was before the body was found.'

'He might have been making his alley good by showing he had nothing to conceal. But about this Scott fellow. He wasn't here when Mrs Gwynne died.'

'We don't *know* that. It's a damned funny thing that he happened to leave just after Gwynne did. He could have been on the car park while Mrs Gwynne was still there and if he was it looks very much as if he might have taken her away and brought her back later.'

'Why bring her back to murder her?'

'I don't say he murdered her, only that he could have gone off with her. Some other man, even Reeves, could have waited for her to come back and murdered her then.'

'We'll have to go into it. Have you got Scott's address?'

'It's on the list there.'

'We'll see him tomorrow. Anybody else likely to be a suspect?'

'Yes. A man named Rodney Fuller. I was asking Alec about him a few minutes ago. He was supposed to be one of Isobel Gwynne's boyfriends and the story is that she ditched him in favour of Scott. Again I don't know how true this is but something I saw myself suggests that there could be something in it.'

The Inspector looked up quickly.

'What was that, Doug?' he asked.

I told Lindon about the little scene I had witnessed from

the annexe bathroom.

'It may be significant or it may not. I wasn't near enough to hear what was said but the gestures suggested that Fuller was asking her for something and she was refusing. I think he tried to grab her, it looked like that, but she pushed him away. She raised her voice at that point and what she said sounded like "Don't be bloody silly".'

'Did it? He could have been pretty mad with her then?'

'It's a point to bear in mind. You see Scott could have taken her away somewhere and brought her back some time after one o'clock. Fuller could have been waiting, furiously jealous at her going off with Scott, and killed her in a fit of rage.'

'That would imply that Fuller knew she'd gone with Scott.'

'He might have just guessed and waited to find out. If so, seeing her with Scott might have just been enough to send Fuller round the bend.'

'That's plausible. It fits.'

'I know. The trouble is that it may have happened the other way round. I don't know where Fuller was at seven o'clock but he could have been hanging round the car park too and gone off with Isobel. I know that it doesn't seem likely in view of what I saw on Saturday afternoon but women do change their minds.'

'You should know,' Lindon said, a little sourly I thought. 'So we've got three possible suspects—Reeves, Scott and Fuller. I suppose a woman couldn't have done this job?'

'I don't think it likely but I wouldn't put it right out of court. The Gwynne woman must have aroused a certain amount of jealousy here and there and she wasn't very big or very robust. But if a woman did it, all that clothes tearing must have been done deliberately to suggest a sexual motive and murder by a man.'

'We'll keep it in mind. Now we'd better get on with the job.'

The Inspector picked up the list of guests and ran his eye down it. This seemed to me to be an appropriate moment to say my piece about Pat and me.

'Bob,' I said. 'There's a girl on the list, a Miss Pat Morland. I think I'd better tell you that during the critical period she was with me.'

Uncle Bob reacted as expected. He was speechless for a good two seconds.

'Well I'm damned,' he said at last. 'There's no doubt about you. Every case we work on you manage to find some accommodating female. Are you telling me that she was with you for several hours at that time of night?'

'Come off your high horse, Bob; Pat and I have known one another for years. It was her suggestion that I come up here for the week-end, she's a regular visitor. The essential point is that we were together from the time the party ended until . . . well, long after the latest time Isobel Gwynne could have been murdered.'

Lindon sighed at his failure to understand the modern generation.

'Well, I suppose she could hardly have a better alibi.'

'She gives me one too you'll notice.'

The Inspector frowned at me, his eyebrows lowered.

'You? You didn't have any truck with that Gwynne woman, did you?'

'No, thank God.'

'All the same, it's just as well you have an alibi, though I must say . . .'

'Don't say it. You were young once.'

'When I was young I didn't hop into bed with every girl I met.'

'No. But I bet you tried.'

'That's enough, Sergeant Gray. I'll have to talk to this Miss Morland. We don't want to give the impression that we have special favourites ... like the girlfriends of over-sexed sergeants.'

'That's all right. She expects it. She won't be embarrassed.'

Lindon shook his head and picked up the list of guests. 'We'll go through this lot in the order they're down here. I can't see any point in changing it. We'll have to talk to everyone anyway.'

We began our long series of interviews with Anne and Peter Randall but they contributed nothing but confirmation that Neville Gwynne had been arguing with his wife at dinner about whether she should go with him to Sydney or not. It was Pat who offered the first bit of useful information. She mentioned a Don Liverson.

'Liverson?' said Lindon. 'I haven't come across that name before.'

'He wasn't a guest, he came to dinner with the Worths on Saturday night and stayed on for the party.'

The Inspector had been handling Pat with a great deal of tact but now he stared at her in a puzzled way.

'Are you telling me that there were people here other than those on this list?'

'Yes. A few of the locals drop in for dinner sometimes.'

'Hell's bells, more of them. Do you happen to know who was here from outside?'

'There weren't very many. Graham and Hazel Worth, Don Liverson and the Mansells. The Worths run the store at Castle Hill and come here often. Don Liverson is Hazel's brother and usually comes too. The Mansells have a property of some kind in the district.'

'All these people stayed right through to the end of the party?'

'Oh yes.'

'Was this Liverson character ever involved with Mrs Gwynne?'

Pat nodded.

'For a while yes, a month or so ago.'

'Was he now? That's interesting. All the same he couldn't have been with Mrs Gwynne if he was at the party though he could have met her later.'

'We can check with the Worths,' I suggested. 'I take it he stays with them?'

'Yes,' said Pat. 'But I think he has his own car.'

'In that case he probably went home independently but the Worths should know when he got back to their place.'

'It looks as if you'll have to stay overnight and question the locals tomorrow,' grumbled Lindon. 'We've got a hell of a lot to do here yet.'

I agreed and suggested to Pat that she try and get a lift back to Sydney with someone else. She said the Randalls would drive her home and went off to arrange it.

We ploughed on. We talked to every guest in the house but only one couple came up with any useful information. A youth named Brian Pollock took a Laurel Prentice for a walk after the party 'because it was such a lovely night and we weren't tired'.

Lindon wasn't very interested until Pollock admitted seeing someone in front of the store shed.

The Inspector almost leapt out of his chair, all seventeen stone of him.

'Who was it? What time was this? Did you recognize anyone?'

Pollock looked bewildered at this barrage.

'Well there were three cars there . . .'

'Cars? What cars?'

'The visitors' cars. The people who came to dinner and stayed on.'

Lindon stared at me.

'Isn't the car park by the annexe?'

'That's for guests only, I think.'

'That's right,' said Pollock. 'Casual visitors always park by the store shed.'

'That adds up,' I said. 'The three cars belonged to the Mansells, the Worths and Don Liverson. Did you see any of them actually drive off?' I asked Pollock.

'No. We just heard someone call out goodnight, I think it was the Worths, and then Laurel and I passed beyond the end of the stables and out of sight.'

Pollock told us that he and his girlfriend got back to the house about twenty past two and saw and heard nothing more.

Lindon let him go.

'This gets sillier and sillier,' said the Inspector as the door closed behind Pollock. 'Nobody took Mrs Gwynne to the store shed while those cars were parked there, that's certain. In my book that means that somebody here murdered her, somebody who was able to watch those cars drive away and knew that the coast was clear. The man she was with during the early part of the evening wouldn't have known when the party was going to end; it might have gone on until two or three in the morning.'

'I think that's it, Bob. She went off on a quiet little frolic with man number one. Man number two waited in a blind fury until she came back, probably about half past one or so, and then took her to the store shed and hanged her. By the time Pollock and his girlfriend got back at two-twenty, Mrs Gwynne was dead and the murderer safely away.'

Lindon scowled.

'Got it made, haven't we? All we have to do is to find two men. Let's get on with it.'

We got on with it. An hour or so later we had finished with the guests and I took the opportunity to say goodnight to Pat. I promised to ring her and let her know what had happened.

I went back to help the Inspector deal with the Strath-wood staff.

4 |

THE staff at Strathwood consisted of first of all a married couple employed as manager and housekeeper. Joe Pearce and his wife Ivy ran the place during the week when Alec was at his sports shop but at the week-end when Alec was present they remained very much in the background. No doubt they had plenty to do, even then. In addition there was a groom, a stable-boy, a cook, four maids and the handyman who had discovered Isobel's body, Jim Saunders. The staff quarters were right at the back of the area surrounding the house and were screened from it by a belt of trees. At the end of the long avenue of trees leading from the road the drive branched, the main drive continuing past the front of the house and then the stables and a slightly narrower path making a circuit round the pool and the tennis court and passing between the back of the annexe and the staff quarters.

Because Pat had wanted to show me the front of the house first, its most engaging aspect, we had driven past it on the main drive and turned right to reach the car park but it could also be reached by taking the longer route and I gathered that casual visitors did just that but instead of stopping at the guests' car park carried on to park in the open space in front of the store shed. This was where the Mansells, the Worths and Don Liverson had parked. I made a rough sketch of the layout for Inspector Lindon's benefit.

We drew a blank with most of the staff, which was to be expected as they made contact with the guests only when their duties demanded it, but one of the maids, a small dark girl in her early twenties, had a highly significant story to tell. This emerged from the routine question by Inspector Lindon as to whether Jenny, the maid, had seen Mrs Gwynne at any time on Saturday night. Jenny took a long time to answer.

'Not on Saturday night,' she volunteered, putting a faint emphasis on the word 'night'.

Something in her manner prompted Lindon to probe further and he encouraged Jenny to give her evidence in her own words. I won't attempt to reproduce them since her eager reluctance to retail a juicy bit of scandal was accompanied by knowing glances and much innuendo but she had overheard Duncan Scott trying to persuade Isobel Gwynne to go to bed with him on Saturday night. Isobel's replies had been non-committal but according to Jenny that didn't mean a thing.

'She was keeping him on a string,' she said confidently.

This conversation had taken place during the afternoon amongst the trees near the yard at the western end of the staff quarters where Jenny was busy hanging out her personal washing and proved so interesting that she had actually peered through a narrow gap in the fence surrounding the yard.

'Your impression is that Mrs Gwynne really intended to spend the night or part of the night with Mr Scott?' Lindon asked.

'Oh, she was going to all right.'

'How do you know that?'

'I could tell by the way she was teasing him. She had him worked up to a fine old state, I can tell you.' Jenny smiled knowingly. 'She wanted him nice and eager.'

Lindon sent Jenny away with a warning to keep quiet about what she had seen and heard, then pushed his chair back and began to fill his pipe.

'That's the best bit of news we've had yet,' he said with satisfaction. 'It's pretty certain that Mrs Gwynne was with Duncan Scott for at least the early part of the evening.'

'It looks like it, but why only the early part? Why didn't he spend the entire night with her?'

'We have only two alternatives, Doug. Either he spent only the evening with her and brought her back for someone else to murder her or he murdered her himself. In either case he must have picked her up from the car park just after Gwynne left or from her cottage a few minutes later.'

'That sounds logical, I admit, but if he just wanted to sleep with the girl why did he take her away?'

Lindon shrugged.

'They didn't want to be seen.'

'Then why bring her back?'

'They had a row.'

'If the row was important enough to provoke murder why didn't he kill her on the spot? Why bring her back to stage that elaborate hanging? There are plenty of places in this area where he could have dumped her body so that it wouldn't be discovered for days . . . perhaps weeks.'

'You like the second man theory better?'

'On the whole, I do. He would have had a classic motive, sexual jealousy, and opportunity to make some preparations.'

'So the second man saw Scott take Isobel away, got madly jealous, fixed up everything in the store shed and just waited for her return? How would he know that she and Scott were coming back at all?'

I shrugged.

'He couldn't know that, of course, but if he was angry enough he would have been prepared to wait all night. That would explain the tearing off of her clothes.'

'Hmm. That fits. So it could be Fuller or Liverson . . . or even Reeves. Where was Reeves around seven o'clock? Could he have seen Mrs Gwynne go off with Scott?'

'I don't see why not. He's in and out of the dining-room during dinner so it might be difficult to discover just where he was at any particular moment.'

The Inspector looked at me doubtfully.

'The evidence against him could be strong, Doug.'

'Don't let that worry you, he's an acquaintance of mine, no more. I'm aware of the evidence. He was in the best position to know what went on here. He knew when Scott left. He could have watched him pick up Isobel from one of several points and of all people he could have moved around without exciting comment. And he knew all about the store shed.'

Lindon nodded.

'We'll keep an open mind about him, we've got a long way to go yet. Let's finish off the rest of the staff.'

We did so but without useful result and just before midnight Lindon packed up and returned to town, taking with him Isobel's clothes, the twine and strap, the chair and the box from the store shed. I went to bed feeling curiously alone amongst all the empty rooms.

On Monday morning I had an early swim in the pool followed by a very large breakfast, and drove off to make my first call. I met with an immediate setback. Mansell was a Pitt Street farmer. In other words he had a business in town and ran a farm under a manager as a tax-saving device, visiting it only at week-ends. Once I was told this I knew where to find him as his firm was one of the largest real estate dealers in Sydney. In Castle Hill I was scarcely any luckier. Don Liverson was not a permanent member of the Worth family but visited them only on occasional week-ends and lived in town. I got his Sydney address and the name of his employers but that was all. I was able to confirm that the Worths, the Mansells and Liverson had all parked their cars in front of the store shed and the Mansells and the Worths had driven away one after the other at about one-fifteen on the Saturday night. They'd seen nothing of Mrs Gwynne and had no idea when Liverson got home since he had his own key and they hadn't waited up for him. They understood he had stayed on to have a last drink with someone.

This statement contained the only possible significant fact I had come across since no one at Strathwood had admitted staying up any later than about one-fifteen to have a last drink with anyone. Liverson's activities might bear investigation.

Back at the house I put a call through to Lindon to tell him I was about to leave for Headquarters and that pleased him as I could now accompany him to visit Scott and Fuller. I had a quick word with Joe Pearce and asked him to keep his eyes and ears open for possible news of Mrs Gwynne in the district in case she and Scott had filled in the early part of the Saturday evening by drinking in one of the local hotels or called on any of the local people. Then I packed my bag and headed back to Sydney.

The Inspector had news for me.

'I've had a preliminary report from Raines,' he said. 'The time of death has narrowed a little. We can take it that Mrs Gwynne died between one and two o'clock on Sunday morning as a working hypothesis but we should allow fifteen minutes either way to be on the safe side.'

'The precise time isn't critical as far as we can tell at the moment.'

'No. But the other bit of news is perhaps more important. Mrs Gwynne hadn't had sexual intercourse before her death.'

I stared.

'She *hadn't*?'

'No. Raines is quite definite on the point. It knocks some of our ideas on the head, doesn't it?'

'It certainly does. What the devil was she doing then?'

'I dunno. All I can suggest is that Scott took her away somewhere and they had a thundering great row so instead of shoving her into bed he hanged her.'

'Well he didn't hang her because she wouldn't play ball if what I've heard about her is correct and I can't imagine

84

any other motive. What I don't understand is why he took her away at all unless he intended to sleep with her.'

'It looks as if our second-man theory holds the field at the moment. He wasn't to know that the early part of the evening had been completely innocent.'

'Yes, but that's tenable only if Scott took her away and brought her back . . .'

'Or someone else took her away and *Scott* waited for her to come back. He would have been the angry man then.'

'The someone else could only have been Fuller . . . unless . . . look Bob, isn't it possible that Gwynne took her away with him and brought her back later? She was away six hours, more or less.'

Lindon shook his head.

'No, Doug. I thought of that. Gwynne was at Mascot at eight-thirty. That's fairly fast driving so he didn't have time to take his wife anywhere. I spoke to Gwynne's client on the phone and he confirmed everything Gwynne said, including the fact that Gwynne left the Wentworth at about one o'clock to go home.'

'One o'clock? In that big Jaguar, at that time of night, Gwynne could have been at Strathwood soon after two . . .'

'Break it down, Doug. I've been too long in this game to accept anyone's word without checking. I put a man on to following Gwynne's movements first thing this morning. Gwynne's Jaguar was in the Wentworth car park from nine-fifteen on Saturday night when he returned from Mascot with his client until nine o'clock Sunday morning when he left to go back to Strathwood. The in and out times and Gwynne's payment for the period are all re-corded. The same constable went on to the Returned Sol-diers League Cab Company and found that Gwynne's trip to the Silver Spade and back and then his journey to Point Piper later were listed and charged to his account. So was his trip down to the Wentworth on Sunday morning. I know this kind of alibi invites suspicion but this one just couldn't have been faked. Too many outsiders are involved.'

'He's definitely in the clear then? He must have left her standing on the car park as he said.'

'I don't think there's any doubt about that. Somebody picked her up from the car park and took her away and we've got to find out who it was. Let's get moving.'

Five hours later we were back in Lindon's office, very much wearier but hardly any wiser. We had interrogated Scott, Fuller, Liverson and Mansell, spending twenty minutes tracking down Scott's and Fuller's business addresses and half an hour eating an indifferent café lunch, much to the Inspector's disgust as he liked his food. I had made a few notes and for our mutual benefit I summarized them briefly. They ran somewhat as follows.

Scott. Scott claimed to know nothing about Mrs Gwynne's death and showed what appeared to be normal surprise. After some preliminary skirmishing he admitted that he had an arrangement with her to meet her after her husband's departure but she had not been on the car park. He assumed that she was waiting for him in her cabin and had driven out of Strathwood, parked his car down the road a little and walked back through the trees only to find Mrs Gwynne's cabin empty. He hung about for a while and then went back to his car and drove home. He claimed to have been a little angry but at the same time relieved. Isobel Gwynne was a demanding but unreliable creature and in many ways he was glad to see the back of her. I put his credibility down at fifty per cent. He may have been speaking the truth but since he lived in a bachelor flat and was able to offer no confirmatory evidence about the time he arrived home he might just as well have been lying.

Fuller. Fuller also swore that he knew nothing about Mrs Gwynne's death and as far as I could tell his surprise when told she had been murdered was genuine. However,

I knew from experience that one couldn't rely on such judgements. Some intensive questioning elicited the fact that he had been intimate with Isobel Gwynne and had been bitter about being dumped in favour of Duncan Scott but he spent the whole of Saturday evening in the hotel at Baulkham Hills, drinking in a private room until one o'clock in the morning and not returning to Strathwood until one-thirty. Pressed by the Inspector, Fuller admitted being fairly drunk by this time and he had gone in search of Mrs Gwynne 'to have it out with her'. Her cabin though had been empty. Frustrated, Fuller had then gone to bed.

I felt inclined to believe Fuller's story but the Inspector disagreed. Superficially Fuller was tailor-made for the part of the murderer as alcohol could have intensified his sense of grievance and engendered a reckless desire to take revenge but I just couldn't see this killing carried out by a fumbling drunk after a solid night's drinking. His alibi for the early part of the evening was probably unshakeable as he certainly wasn't drinking alone and he could have had no knowledge of where Isobel Gwynne had gone or when she was due to return. Wandering over to her cottage to have it out with her was the typical act of a man fuddled by drink. His final words, however, interested the Inspector and me. He claimed to have heard a car drive off from in front of the store shed about a quarter past two. Since his room was in the annexe the statement sounded reasonable and the car must have been Liverson's.

Liverson. Fuller's evidence had made us particularly keen to interview Liverson since he had been hanging round Strathwood as late as two-fifteen, close to the upper limit of Dr Raines' time bracket and it seemed highly unlikely that anyone, apart from Liverson himself, would have taken Mrs Gwynne to the store shed while his car was still parked in front of it. He turned out to be a brash, talkative salesman and told his story with supreme confidence. At one o'clock the Dentons, the couple who occupied the cottage furthest from the main building, had invited him over for a nightcap and so as not to be odd man out he had persuaded a girl, a Joan Tyler, to join him. Another couple, the Connells, had also been present. Knowing that his statement could be checked he said that he had taken Miss Tyler back to her room at about one-thirty or a little later. His confidence sagged a little when Lindon pointed out that we had evidence that his car didn't leave until two-fifteen. His explanation was that he and Miss Tyler had dallied a little on their way from the Denton's cottage. 'She'd had a few drinks and was asking for it,' he said defensively, typically blaming the woman. To Inspector Lindon's disgust this gave Liverson a fair alibi as Miss Tyler had shared a room with another girl who would no doubt confirm the time Miss Tyler returned.

Mansell. The call on Mansell was a mere formality. He confirmed that he and his wife had driven away from Strathwood at one-fifteen, immediately after the Worths. They had seen or heard nothing in any way unusual.

'One thing strikes me as a little odd,' I said, as I closed my notebook.

'Only one?' growled Lindon.

'Well, one for a start. That was the number of people moving about the place at the time Mrs Gwynne was murdered. There was Brian Pollock and his girlfriend, Fuller after he got back from Baulkham Hills, Liverson and Miss Tyler and for all we know Duncan Scott. The murderer must have run a hell of a risk carrying Isobel Gwynne to the store shed.'

'There were gaps, Doug. Liverson, for example was nowhere near the store shed between one o'clock and two-fifteen. That's more than an hour.'

'Yes, but the murderer couldn't know he was going to have that long. Liverson could have turned up to collect his car at any moment.'

'But damn it all, Doug,' said Lindon impatiently, 'Mrs Gwynne was murdered between one and two. We can't get away from that. Somebody grabbed her, clapped a hand over her mouth to stop her yelling and carried her to that shed. Of course there was some risk but somebody chanced it and got away with it.'

'Then where was she when she was grabbed?'

'How the devil should I know? Obviously there's something wrong with all this evidence and we've got to find out what it is. We'll have to check those alibis for a start. I'm not taking anybody's word for granted. You can chase up that Tyler woman and get confirmation of Liverson's story and you might have a go at the Dentons and the Connells while you're about it. On Sunday night they told us they'd gone straight to bed after the party.'

'I suppose they thought that as they were tucked away in a cabin that was good enough.'

'Well it isn't good enough. Then there's Fuller's yarn about drinking at Baulkham Hills, that will have to be checked. I don't know what we can do about Scott but it's possible that other tenants in the flats where he lives heard him come home. If it was as late as say three o'clock he'll have some explaining to do.'

'What about the possibility that someone not at Strathwood went there on Saturday night just to murder Isobel Gwynne. It doesn't have to be someone actually staying there.'

Lindon resisted this outrageous idea.

'It's out of the question. Someone up there did it.'

'Look, Bob,' I said earnestly, 'I know these alibis have got to be checked but I'm very much afraid that after I've done that we are going to be exactly where we are now. Eventually we are going to have to consider the possibility that someone from outside used Strathwood simply as a screen. It could have been done.'

'All right. Talk to Reeves and your girlfriend and see

what you can find out about Mrs Gwynne's private life. At the same time you can do something about verifying Reeves' own statement. He was in a perfect position to murder Mrs Gwynne.'

'I'll talk to him. And maybe run out to Strathwood again.'

I went back to my own little office.

5 |

WITH an uncomfortable feeling that I was wasting my time I sat down and scribbled out a rough programme. Checking alibis was, quite rightly, standard practice, but in my opinion every rule ought to be applied with a little common sense. I really couldn't see any point in chasing out to Baulkham Hills for example because Fuller wouldn't have made a statement involving other people unless it were true. The essential part of his evidence was just that part which couldn't be checked, that which related to his movements after he returned to Strathwood in the early hours of the morning. However, I had to carry out orders.

Fortunately there were one or two people I could deal with that evening, Scott for a start. He lived at Elizabeth Bay and from there it was only a short run to Miss Tyler's home at Double Bay. So far so good. But the Dentons and the Connells were a plain, unvarnished nuisance, the Dentons living at Hurstville on the other side of the city and the Connells miles away at Turramurra. Despite Lindon's instructions, I decided to ignore them for the moment. If Joan Tyler confirmed Liverson's story then their evidence would be redundant and I didn't feel like driving fifty miles to tell them they'd been naughty in deceiving the Inspector. I looked down at the list of guests with distaste. There were thirty-one names, including those of the people who came only for the evening. All of them had told their stories and I doubted very much whether any of them would have anything to add.

Checking on Fuller's drinking bout I'd have to leave until tomorrow. I supposed I'd have to do it, though I was quite sure the effort would result in no more than a pleasant trip into the country. But there was one couple I would talk to, mainly because they lived at Paddington and

I could call on them on my way back from Double Bay. Their room had been in the main building so it was faintly possible that they might have something to say about Alec Reeves' movements. It wasn't likely, but a visit to them would ease my conscience and maybe satisfy Inspector Lindon.

I had dinner in the canteen and then set off, visiting Scott first. This was a complete washout. He lived in a block of flats roughly designed on the rabbit-warren principle and the notion that any one inhabitant took any notice of the comings and goings of any other merely provoked polite amusement when I asked a few questions. Even the arrival of his car drew no attention since he kept it in the street. He stuck to his story and his credibility remained at fifty per cent. Somewhat dispiritedly I drove on to Double Bay.

I interviewed Miss Tyler on the doorstep of her comfortable home until our conversation reached a critical point. She had freely admitted going to the Dentons' cabin with Don Liverson but at first insisted that he took her back to her room at half past one. At this point I suggested that she might like to accompany me to my car where we could talk without being overheard by her parents. She agreed very reluctantly, guessing the kind of question I was now obliged to ask her. I told her we had evidence that Liverson remained at Strathwood until a quarter past two, that he had claimed that he had spent the last forty-five minutes with her and it was essential that we know the truth. I also added artfully that her room-mate, Beryl Edwards, would know the time she returned. She gave in. I didn't press her for details but took her back to her front gate and assured her that it was unlikely she would have to go into court and confess her misdeeds.

So Liverson was cleared. I supposed that that was something gained yet something had been lost also in the sense that Miss Tyler's and Liverson's presence in the area at the critical time made it even more difficult to understand the murderer's movements. Before I stopped her confession Joan Tyler had told me that she and Liverson had not gone very far for their love-making, they had parked themselves on the grass a little beyond the line of cabins so they couldn't have been any great distance from Mrs Gwynne's cottage. This suggested that the murder had taken place between one o'clock and one-thirty. During that time all the likely witnesses were far afield, Fuller not yet returned from Baulkham Hills, Pollock and Miss Prentice were still out in the woods and Liverson was with Joan Tyler in the Dentons' cabin. That left Alec Reeves. I drove to the Randalls.

The Randalls lived in a remodelled terrace house, all off-white paint and window-boxes. It was very charming but too much like a doll's house for my taste. They told me that the regular visitors to Strathwood formed a fairly tight bunch, riding together, playing tennis, swimming in the pool and of course drinking. But none of them had any contact with each other outside Strathwood.

'I was a little surprised to find people like the Gwynnes there at all,' I said. 'Isobel didn't appear to do anything very much. I just couldn't imagine her on a horse.'

'Not Isobel,' said Anne. 'She was a real hothouse plant. But Neville's quite a good rider; and not a bad tennis player either.'

'You surprise me.'

'Don't be fooled by his slightly foppish manner. He's very conscious of his image as a with-it advertising man, hence the Jaguar, the expense account and his expensive taste in grog. I think he could be quite tough, if necessary.'

'He didn't seem very tough where Isobel was concerned.'

Anne smiled.

'Every man has his weakness. Actually Neville was

93

rather proud of having married a girl whom every man wanted. I think he saw her little affairs as proof of his own superiority.'

'But surely he must have suspected that these little affairs, as you call them, ended up in bed?'

'I don't think he did. His ego was too big for him to believe that Isobel would sleep with anyone other than him.'

I probed around for information about the Gwynnes' activities outside Strathwood but the Randalls knew nothing about their private lives apart from the fact that Neville was in advertising and Isobel ran a dress shop. I wasn't any luckier with questions about Alec Reeves. Peter explained that during the night there were often small noises, people going to the bathroom after a night of fairly solid drinking and that sort of thing. Alec could have left his room at any time after about one-fifteen without exciting comment.

I took the police car back to Headquarters, swapped it for my own and went home. My evening hadn't been very productive. Neither was Tuesday morning. A visit to the Baulkham Hills Hotel confirmed that Rodney Fuller had spent Saturday evening drinking. The publican, who knew Fuller, explained that a bunch of 'the boys' had rented a room and stayed on until about one o'clock. The sale of liquor after ten o'clock was prohibited by law but a man could drink all night in his own room, providing he bought the liquor before ten. I wasn't fooled by the renting claim but I wasn't there to police the licensing laws so I accepted the story for what it was worth, which wasn't much. It simply showed that Isobel Gwynne hadn't been with Fuller during the early part of the evening. The case was tightening up. I was becoming convinced that some outside agency was involved. Isobel hadn't been with Scott, or at least she hadn't had intercourse with him which seemed to come to the same thing, she hadn't been with Fuller, she hadn't been with Liverson and she hadn't been with Reeves. She hadn't dematerialized into an astral body so she must have left Strathwood, willingly or unwillingly, with someone from outside. Either they brought her back and murdered her or they brought her back in time for someone at Strathwood to murder her. In any case I had to find out where she had been since that seemed to be the key to the fact that she had been stripped and hanged in the early hours of Sunday morning.

I had better go and see Alec Reeves. He would surely know something about the Gwynnes' private life. I headed for Castlereagh Street.

'Alec,' I said to him as we sat in his office at the back of his sports shop amongst the cricket bats, tennis rackets, fishing gear and golf clubs. 'Do you know anything about the Gwynnes' background?'

'Not much, Doug. I know that Neville's an advertising man and that Isobel ran, or helped to run, a dress shop of some kind but that's about all.'

This wasn't a very auspicious start but I persisted.

'Haven't you ever come across any of their personal friends? Didn't they ever bring anyone to Strathwood?'

Alec frowned.

'Well yes, they did, now you come to mention it. A couple of times.'

'Can you remember the names of these people?'

'Only of one couple and I remember them because the week-end wasn't a particular success. It was the woman who ran the dress shop with Isobel and her husband, a couple named Thatcher.'

'Why do you say the week-end wasn't a success?'

'Well, the Thatchers didn't seem to fit in with the sort of crowd we get at Strathwood. They didn't ride, they didn't play tennis. All they did was to sit around looking decorative . . . and drinking. They were pretty good at that.'

'I suppose they were very close friends of the Gwynnes

if the two women ran a shop together?'

'I've no idea, Doug. I imagine the women must have known one another fairly well.'

'Where is this dress shop? Do you know?'

'Yes. It's at Double Bay. A place called the Bird Cage.'

'The Bird Cage?'

Alec smiled.

'It's done up like a gilded cage, I gather, one of these boutique places.'

'You can't remember anyone else who came with the Gwynnes to Strathwood?'

'I wouldn't have a clue, Doug. Do you know how many people have visited the place over the last couple of years?'

'I've no idea. But it's something I might be interested in.'

'I'm not absolutely sure myself but I know it's something like seven or eight hundred. That includes the family groups who come up at Easter and times like that.'

'Oh Lord. As many as that?'

'It could be more. But why are you interested?'

'I'll tell you in a moment. What about the regulars? People who come every week-end or nearly every week-end. Do you know how many that would be?'

'That's a damned difficult question to answer. They come and go. Some people come regularly for a few months and then drop out and others replace them. The crowd changes all the time.'

'But say over the last three months? Or maybe six months?'

Alec grinned wryly.

'You do make it difficult. How does one define a regular? Some people come two or three times a month, some every other week for a whole year. I should say at a rough guess that about sixty or seventy could be considered regular guests, maybe another twenty or so fairly regular. I get about thirty to forty people a week but of course the numbers drop considerably during a spell of bad weather. But look, Doug, if you tell me what you are after I might be of more use.'

This was one of the difficulties of dealing with people one knew and with someone I should be busily suspecting of murder. But I had to balance the risks of confiding in a possible suspect against the prospect of getting useful information. I decided to take a chance.

'It's like this, Alec. I am becoming convinced that nobody who was at Strathwood last week-end had anything to do with Isobel Gwynne's murder. I can't go into details and what I've said doesn't mean that everyone who was there is cleared completely but it's beginning to look as if someone went up during the evening specially to deal with Isobel. You see what that means, don't you? It had to be someone who was highly familiar with the place and who also knew that Neville Gwynne was going to be away on Saturday night. In short, someone who knew the Gwynnes and had also been a visitor to Strathwood.'

'Hell. That's a tall order, isn't it? The only people I know who would fit into that category are the Thatchers. How well they knew Strathwood I couldn't guess but as they were hanging round the place for an entire week-end they could know about the store shed and the Saturday night routine. But for all I know quite a number of people had some contact with the Gwynnes outside Strathwood.'

'That's the trouble. How about getting me a list of the regular visitors over the last six months?'

'I can give you a list of *all* the visitors. That would be easy but separating them out into regular and casual would be too difficult. I'll have to give Joe Pearce a ring and ask him to make out a list as he has all the records up there. What I can do is to ask him to mark against each name the number of times each person had been to Strathwood then you can decide which of them is worth investigating.'

'My guess is that we'll end up investigating the whole damned lot,' I said gloomily. 'But that's our problem. One thing you might be able to tell me. Who brought the Gwynnes to Strathwood in the first place? Or did they just see an advertisement?'

'No. They came originally with a couple named Elwood, if I remember rightly. It's nearly a year ago though.'

'Do the Elwoods still go to Strathwood?'

'No. Elwood got transferred to Melbourne, I think. At any rate they haven't been there for at least six months.'

In one way my talk with Alec Reeves had been extremely depressing. The idea of interviewing God knows how many people looking for links with the Gwynnes was too appalling, the chief snag being that if one of them had murdered Isobel he wasn't going to hand us a written confession. There would have to be cross-checking and patient unravelling of hundreds of bits of evidence, most of it trivial. One didn't get information directly from a murderer, at least not very often, but from people who knew him and knew what he had done, where he had been and when. As for links with the Gwynnes, I might have to rely on Neville himself, though in this context a husband would be a shaky reed. Obviously someone had wanted to murder Isobel and had done so but equally obviously he hadn't known of this threat or he would have taken steps to protect her. The very nature of murder makes it necessary for no one to know of the murderer's intention.

But my perennially suspicious detective's mind was already starting to wrap my outsider theory around Mr and Mrs Thatcher. Lindon, of course, would scoff like mad at the very idea of building what he would call fancy theories without any evidence but in many ways the Thatchers fitted my hypothetical case perfectly. For a start there was a possible motive, a motive second only to sex as a trigger for murder. Money. If there had been any funny business with the financial side of running this Bird Cage place the Thatchers might well have wanted Isobel out of the way. This was a wildly speculative notion but not a wildly improbable one. I knew there were enough arguments and fights about money to make such a thing possible.

If Isobel and Mrs Thatcher had worked together for any length of time the latter would certainly know that the Gwynnes intended to spend the week-end at Strathwood and would probably know that Neville had to return to Sydney on Saturday night. Having been to Strathwood they might well have known about the store shed and what it contained, especially as they apparently did nothing but hang around the immediate vicinity of the house. They could have known which cabin the Gwynnes were going to occupy and they'd also know that between dinner and the time the Saturday party got going, about eight o'clock, Isobel would most likely be alone in her cabin because that was the time when women gave final touches to their make-up and made preparations for the evening's festivities.

There were any number of ways of getting into Strathwood unseen, particularly to the cottages which were set amongst trees. I remembered too that a path ran from the main road alongside the race track which brought one to the drive at a point by the end of the stables and quite near the store shed and the car park. Had they been fortunate enough to have found Isobel on the car park they could have whisked her away without very much risk of discovery. And that brought me to another interesting point. Both Lindon and I had given some thought to the problem facing the murderer in getting Isobel into the store shed. My first idea had been that the murderer had clapped a hand over her mouth and carried her kicking and struggling to the store shed door, shoved her inside and then gagged and bound her. But this could have happened only if his original attack on her had taken place somewhere fairly near the store shed. Carrying her any distance would have been dangerous, she had only to get her mouth free for an instant to let out a scream that would have brought half of Strathwood running to her aid. During my police career I had handled enough drunk and disorderly females to know that an active woman was a big enough handful even without having to use one hand to keep her quiet.

The alternative was that the murderer had gagged and bound her somewhere else, possibly in her cabin, and carried her like an inert bundle to the store shed. I now thought how much easier this process would be with two people at work. Moreover, the actual physical task of suspending her from the rafter would have been more easily accomplished by two people rather than one. Even the act of stripping Isobel's clothes from her body fell into place, it was just as likely to have been the work of a vicious, and possibly jealous, woman as that of a man.

Finally the fact that Isobel hadn't had sexual intercourse, hadn't had food or drink and hadn't been seen at Strathwood after about ten to seven could be explained on the assumption that she had been abducted, held somewhere and later brought back to be hanged. Of course the theory had holes in it. If the Thatchers or anybody else had wanted to murder Isobel and had her in their clutches as early as seven o'clock why had they waited until half past one in the morning? But they did wait and the reason must have been that, knowing Isobel's proclivities, they decided to make the murder look like the work of some sexually jealous male and chose a time when a number of men could come under suspicion.

Unsupported as my argument was, I thought the possibility well worth investigating. In any case we had now come to a halt and our next move must be to widen the field of our inquiries. I could see only three ways to do that. One, to embark on the tortuous process of interrogating the dozens and dozens of people who had been to Strathwood over the last six months, which was an arbitrary period anyway; the murderer's knowledge of Strathwood could have dated back a year or earlier. Two, question Neville Gwynne and try and learn from him who would have been likely to have murdered his wife; a forlorn hope that, I guessed. I had already decided that Gwynne would have taken some action had he known of a threat to his wife but added to that was the certainty that the murderer would have taken care to see that Gwynne didn't become suspicious. Three, to interview somebody who could give me some information about Isobel's background apart from her visits to Strathwood. Since Mrs Thatcher was the only person we had come across likely to be able to do that, a move in her direction was fully justified. Having thus found an excuse to go my own way I proceeded to Head-quarters.

Lindon wasn't in so I rang Pat and invited her to dinner instead of lunch. She was delighted and I arranged to pick her up at seven. I asked her what she knew of the Thatchers but she was able to tell me only that Mrs Thatcher's Christian name was Muriel. A great help. She knew that the Bird Cage was a shop but how big it was and how valuable she couldn't say. Isobel always seemed to be expensively dressed and apparently affluent so there could be quite a lot of money involved. It might be worth a murder, I decided.

It was now getting near lunch-time but before attempting to satisfy my growing pangs of hunger I put a call through to our financial section and asked them whether they could find out anything about the Bird Cage, jointly owned, as far as I knew, by Isobel Gwynne and Muriel Thatcher. I thought it possible that the shop might be registered as a private company with both husbands and wives as shareholders. I got the department's reply when I came back from lunch and it was interesting. There was a company registered as the Bird Cage Proprietary Limited but it had only two directors, Muriel Thatcher and Isobel Gwynne. It had been formed two years ago. It was a private company and there was no record of its having been listed in the bankruptcy court or prosecuted for tax evasion or found guilty of any breach of the Companies Act. In short, nothing to bring it to the notice of any authority.

If I wanted to know any more it looked as if I should have to see Neville Gwynne, get my hands on Isobel's private papers and contact the company solicitors. It looked rather as if the two women were anxious to keep their husbands out of their business affairs but I wondered what was going to happen to Isobel's share now that she was dead. I presumed that Neville would get it so the best thing to do was to go and see him.

Neville Gwynne's office was in North Sydney. I telephoned him first to make sure he was going to be in and made an appointment for the early afternoon. Inspector Lindon came in before I left and somewhat tentatively I put my ideas to him. Exactly as expected, he accused me of building airy-fairy theories out of nothing. We usually had a battle of this kind at some point during a case but this time Uncle Bob had run out of ammunition. There didn't seem to be anything further we could do for the moment about our current suspects. It seemed essential that we should find out where Isobel Gwynne had been for the six hours or so after her husband had left and for that period Reeves, Fuller and Liverson had incontestable alibis. Scott was the only doubtful one and even in his case the chances seemed slim. He wouldn't have left her had he been with her earlier. The Inspector gave in.

'I suppose you'd better go ahead,' he said in the end. 'At least it will show we're not neglecting any possibility.'

I drove to North Sydney hopefully.

The foyer of Braidwood Advertising shrieked soft sell in a voice of muted thunder. It was a large imposing area decorated entirely in off-white, the carpet, the walls, the ceiling and the receptionist's hair. She was a bleached blonde. There was an off-white table, very low, with four off-white chairs and even an off-white reception desk. The only colour was provided by an off-white framed modern painting, the magazines on the table and the exquisite make-up on the receptionist's face. And I almost forgot, the firm's name in very discreet old gold.

I crossed the deep-piled carpet, asked for Mr Gwynne and was treated to a dazzling smile. After all I *might* have been a client. I was then asked the usual question, said that I had an appointment and gave my name but not my occupation. My request was relayed through the chain of command and ultimately reached Gwynne. An elegant brunette came into the foyer and personally escorted me into the presence. I should have been wearing a new suit.

Gwynne looked a very different figure in an office clearly designed to impress and totally unlike the sad specimen of humanity he had seemed when I last saw him. Naturally the large office, the large desk and the comfortable visitors' chairs, plus the studied elegance of the surroundings added a little to his stature but the way he stood up, moved round the desk and came forward to shake my hand showed me a different side to his character. The successful business executive. He asked me to sit down and then dropped into a visitor's chair beside me. He opened the conversation.

'I suppose you haven't come to tell me you've made some progress in finding my wife's murderer?' he said.

I didn't actually smile but I relaxed my features sufficiently to indicate how absurd I thought the question.

'It depends on what you call progress. We have cleared the ground a little but there are some very puzzling features about your wife's death.'

'I can appreciate that. As you've probably guessed I've thought of little else during the last couple of days and I just can't imagine anybody wanting to kill Isobel. It just doesn't make sense.'

'I won't go into details but the trend of our investigations strongly suggests that the motive for her murder rested in something outside Strathwood.'

'Outside Strathwood? But she was killed ...'

'Yes, I know. We appreciate that her assailant can only have been someone familiar with Strathwood but we have some reason to believe that he made a special trip there on Saturday night. In a sense the murderer made use of Strathwood in order to suggest that your wife had been killed by somebody there. This is where we need your help.'

'My help? What can I do?'

'You can give us the names of every person who has been to Strathwood with you. That is, the names of people who know the place, yet who had some relationship with you independently of Strathwood.'

Gwynne frowned and shook his head.

'I don't like that at all,' he said. 'Frankly I find the idea of any of my friends being concerned in Isobel's murder extremely distasteful. That is what you are saying, isn't it?'

'Not exactly. But even you, as a layman, will understand that there has to be some close connection between a murderer and his victim. People don't kill total strangers, except possibly when someone goes insane. That's pretty rare.'

'I wouldn't say that. Where a woman is concerned, especially an attractive woman like Isobel, a strange man could be concerned. Was she ... was she assaulted?'

'No. She wasn't.'

'Well then, couldn't her murderer have killed her because she wouldn't give in to him?'

I hesitated.

'Mr Gwynne, I'm not sure that I like discussing this

aspect of the matter with you. It could be very distressing.'

'Oh no. No. I assure you. I have only one thought in mind, to bring this devil to justice. I've got over my original shock. If there's anything I can do to help . . .'

'Possibly you can. But let's deal with your suggestion first. It seems to me very unlikely that an attacker would go as far as killing a woman who wouldn't give in to him, he wouldn't have any need to. Your wife wasn't a very big woman nor very robust so any normally-built man would have had no difficulty in forcing her submission. Not only that, had she fought so energetically that her assailant lost his temper he would have throttled her on the spot, not taken her to the store shed.'

'Well, I don't want to teach you your job, Sergeant, but to me my wife's murder looked like the work of a sexual maniac. Haven't you considered the possibility that he did throttle her on the spot and then dumped her body in the store shed to delay discovery?'

Gwynne's question put me in a difficulty. He didn't know that Isobel had been stripped and hanged and I wondered whether I should tell him. Later I intended to ask him about the people he had taken to Strathwood and about the Thatchers particularly or anyone else who might conceivably have had a reason for wanting to murder his wife. To do that without diffidence he would need to know that the person who murdered Isobel did so deliberately and brutally. What made the problem worse was the fact that he appeared not to know that Isobel had been something close to a nymphomaniac and the consequent likelihood that her murder resulted from her sexual activities. I decided to skate around the question if I possibly could.

'We have very good reason to believe that your wife wasn't murdered by some tramp or other man wandering around Strathwood in the dark. We believe that her death resulted from a carefully planned attack by someone who knew a great deal about your movements and hers.'

'I don't believe it,' said Gwynne with spirit.

'You don't believe what, Mr Gwynne?'

'That Isobel had that sort of enemy. You say she wasn't killed by some casual tramp. What makes you so sure? Anybody could have walked into that place. I simply won't believe that someone we knew killed her. That's what you said before.'

'Mr Gwynne,' I said slowly. 'I'm afraid I am going to be brutally frank. I didn't want to tell you this but I think it is now necessary for you to know that your wife was stripped and hanged. It was an act of punishment or revenge, not the work of some crazy rapist.'

Gwynne put his hands to his head.

'My God, I don't understand it. Why should anyone want to do such a horrible thing? Isobel hadn't an enemy in the world.'

'I know how you must feel but you must understand that we need your help. We are up against this problem. Either, as I suggested, someone hated your wife so much that he committed this act of vengeance or the whole thing was deliberately staged to make it appear that her murder had some sexual basis. Personally I am inclined to accept the latter view but, as you can see, it entails some other kind of motive.'

'This takes an awful lot of swallowing. I don't want to point a finger at anyone but there were a lot of men at Strathwood.'

'We've virtually eliminated everyone at Strathwood. Let me be brutally frank again. When an attractive woman is murdered, particularly in circumstances like these, it is very easy to assume that some half-crazed sexual maniac has been at work. But your wife wasn't criminally assaulted and since we have investigated all the likely possibilities at Strathwood itself we are now obliged to consider alternatives. The obvious one is that someone went to Strathwood last Saturday evening either with the deliberate intention of murdering your wife or for some reason that ultimately led to her death. Now this clearly involves someone who knew the place well, knew that your wife was going to be alone and could plan accordingly. I am now asking you whether you can name anyone who would fall into this category.'

Gwynne shook his head.

'Look, Sergeant, I know I said I'd help you but I can't go along with this. I can't imagine anybody going out to Strathwood just to murder Isobel. In fact none of my friends would have much interest in Strathwood.' He smiled faintly. 'I'm afraid they'd rather sit on a stool in the Chevron Bar than on a horse.'

'But you have taken people to Strathwood?'

'Well, yes. A couple of times.'

'Who were they?'

'Once we took some people named Westleigh but they wouldn't interest you. Westleigh was a client of mine at one stage but we've since lost the account and I haven't made any contact with him for months.'

'And you also took the Thatchers, I believe.'

'The Thatchers? You surely don't suspect them?'

This was where I had to tread delicately. If the Thatchers had any motive for killing Isobel it would almost certainly be a financial one and I wasn't sure how far Gwynne himself was involved. If he'd had no interest in the shop before, he probably had one now and I had to rely on him for information. I could have the affairs of the Bird Cage investigated but only if I had some reason to suspect some dirty work behind the scenes.

'I have been told that Mrs Thatcher ran a dress shop with your wife.'

'That is true.'

'Does that mean that the business was owned jointly by your wife and Mrs Thatcher?'

'Yes.'

'Did you own any shares in it?'

'No, I didn't. My wife had some money of her own and she used it to start the Bird Cage. She insisted that she wanted some interest outside the home apart from me so I had nothing to do with it.'

'I take it that your wife's share has passed to you?'

'To tell you the truth I haven't had much time to think about it. Isobel and I had wills that left everything to each other so it's possible that I now own half of the Bird Cage though that is by no means certain. I don't know what kind of agreement there was between Isobel and Muriel.'

'But surely, as your wife's heir, you would have inherited her share of the business?'

'Not necessarily. Isobel provided most of the capital but Muriel had the expert knowledge and the trade contacts and I'm sure she would have insisted on some protection against the possibility that Isobel would sell her share to someone who knew nothing about running dress shops. Someone like that with a half-share and who interfered in the running of the shop could wreck it in a few months. But you are not suggesting that Muriel had any part in my wife's death?'

'I'm not suggesting anything but I am obliged to investigate every possibility.'

'But the idea's absurd.'

'It may seem so to you but the Thatchers may well have gained by your wife's death. Can you say for certain that they have not?'

'No. I'm afraid I can't. On the other hand I don't see how they could have.'

'That remains to be seen. Were you friendly with the Thatchers?'

'Not particularly.'

'Was your wife on friendly terms with Muriel Thatcher?'

'As far as I know she was but I wouldn't care to make any assertions where women are concerned. You know what they are like, fighting like scalded cats one minute, as thick as thieves the next.'

'They must have been fairly close since they formed a company together. Or was their relationship strictly business?'

Gwynne looked up sharply.

'You have already started to investigate my wife's business affairs?'

'I've made certain inquiries, yes. The point about the formation of the company is that your wife must have had some personal papers somewhere. Would they be at your flat?'

'I suppose so. I mean, I know she had papers of some kind but whether they included business papers I couldn't say. I think it more likely that these were kept in the office at the Bird Cage.'

'I doubt it. Each partner would have copies of the articles of association and any special agreement between them, so I must ask you to let me have whatever papers you can find.'

'I'll dig them out.'

'Thank you. Do you know who the company's solicitors are?'

'Yes. A fellow named Crouch from Mather, Mather and Crouch.'

'Is he your solicitor too?'

'Oh no. Isobel and I used a different firm for our private work. All the affairs of the company were kept quite separate.'

I made a note of the company solicitor's name. It might pay me to have a talk with him. I changed the subject, or rather moved to another aspect of it.

'When did you take the Thatchers to Strathwood?'

'About a couple of months ago, I suppose.'

'They've never been back there?'

'No. They didn't care for it. Not their cup of tea.'

'Mrs Thatcher would know that you and your wife were regular visitors to Strathwood?'

'Oh yes.'

'So she knew you were going there last week-end?'

'I should think it highly likely.'

'Would she have also known that you had to return to Sydney on Saturday night?'

'That's something I can't answer but again I think it quite possible. No doubt Isobel and Muriel discussed their social activities in great detail. Most women do.'

'I suppose so. Now there's one other matter I want to discuss with you. Your wife died during the early hours of Sunday morning but she was missing from the time you left her on the car park at Strathwood. So far we haven't been able to trace her movements. Did she give you any indication of where she might be going?'

'Why should she? I assumed that she was going to the party. That was her intention.'

'Well she wasn't at the party and as far as we can ascertain she wasn't with anyone from Strathwood. This is one of the most puzzling features of the case and one of the reasons I am making inquiries elsewhere.'

'I think you are quite wrong, Sergeant. In my opinion the answer to the problem will be found at Strathwood. I don't want to accuse anybody, but that fellow Scott had been paying her a lot of attention.'

'I know. But we've investigated that aspect of the matter very thoroughly and it seems fairly certain that Mrs Gwynne wasn't with Scott. The question is do you know of anyone she could have spent the early hours of the evening with? Local people, for example?'

'The only local people we knew were those who came to dinner occasionally. We had nothing to do with them outside Strathwood.'

'You didn't visit any of their homes?'

'No, never.'

'The whole thing's extremely puzzling. If we can dis-cover where your wife went we might have a better chance of finding her murderer.'

'Well all I can say, Sergeant, is that I hope you don't worry the Thatchers too much. I haven't had much to do with them up till now but I am going to have to talk to Muriel about the financial affairs of the Bird Cage and it could be damned awkward for me.'

6

THE bleached blonde gave me a dazzling smile as I padded my way through the deep carpet of the foyer but it brightened my life only momentarily. I was beginning to lose some of my enthusiasm for the Thatcher theory. Somehow it just didn't seem likely that a couple would embark on murder just to gain control of a shop. And it had to be a couple. Muriel Thatcher couldn't have engineered Isobel's death alone and what did the male Thatcher get out of it? Also, I was a little puzzled about how to go about getting information. The first thing, I guessed, was to determine whether the Thatchers had been physically able to murder Isobel. If they had alibis for Saturday night my whole case against them automatically collapsed. On the other hand I couldn't demand alibis without reasonable suspicion that they had been involved.

By the time I reached Headquarters I had made up my mind to call on the solicitor who had organized the company for the two women. If it was a cast-iron arrangement that made it impossible for one woman to swindle the other then I could forget the whole thing since the Thatchers would have had no motive. I rang Crouch as soon as I got in.

As usual with solicitors he made difficulties but equally as usual I countered them with a threat to get the necessary authority to delve deeply into Isobel's financial affairs, something that always horrifies men of the law. I was in his office in Hunter Street fifteen minutes later. He was a youngish man in an oldish office and once he'd said his patter about the sanctity of client confidences and solicitor's responsibilities he was quite co-operative.

'Without going into detail, my clients formed an ordinary private company with a normal capital and equal shares, Mrs Thatcher being the governing director,'

Crouch said.

'So Mrs Thatcher was the governing director? What exactly does that mean?'

Crouch smiled a little.

'The powers of the governing director are all set out clearly in the articles of association. At least you may not consider them very clear as they are described in legal phraseology but in effect she ran the business.'

'But the two women had equal shares you say?'

'Oh yes. Mrs Thatcher as governing director earned a little higher salary than Mrs Gwynne but all profits and accumulated capital gains were shared between them.'

'That seems to be clear enough but the question I am most interested in is what happens to Mrs Gwynne's shares now that she is dead?'

'Ah, I thought you might want to know that. Before the company was formed Mrs Thatcher and Mrs Gwynne had an agreement by which in the event of one of them wishing to pull out, the remaining partner had first option on the other's share of the business. The same thing applied in the case of one of them dying. Substantially, this arrangement has been incorporated into the articles of the company. The idea behind this is that the shares must always remain within the control of the company. The surviving partner can take up the option or not as she pleases but she has the right to buy the shares at an independent valuation if she wishes. In other words, Mrs Gwynne's shares probably now belong to her widower, I don't know the terms of her will, of course, but he must sell to Mrs Thatcher if she wants to buy them.'

'Who makes this independent valuation?'

'The company auditor, in this case.'

'Is there any time limit on this option?'

'Well yes. First there will be a company meeting at which a new director will be appointed to fill Mrs Gwynne's place. It may be Mr Gwynne or it may be Mr

Thatcher though it could be some total stranger, stranger to me I mean. The decision to take up the option or not will be made then and the offer made within twenty-eight days.'

'Assuming Gwynne is his wife's heir must he sell his shares?'

'Oh yes. These are shares in a private company, not negotiable stock. The company must approve all sales so he couldn't dispose of them to someone else. By the same token he can only keep them with the approval of the company, that is if the company doesn't take up the option. Of course I have no idea what Mrs Thatcher's plans are. She may well decided to welcome Mr Gwynne as the new director or admit both Gwynne and her husband as directors.'

'This seems an awful lot of rigmarole for one small shop.'

'Small shop? Whatever gave you that idea?'

'I thought it was one of these little boutique places.'

Crouch laughed.

'It might have been once. It's two storeys now and half a dozen departments. It sells everything a woman needs, and a great many things she doesn't need, if you ask me.'

'It's a profitable business then?'

'You can say that again. Now Kenworthy's want it it's worth a fortune.'

I stared at Crouch. Kenworthy's was an enormous organization with department stores all over the place.

'Are you saying that Kenworthy's want to buy the Bird Cage?'

Crouch hesitated.

'Didn't you tell me over the phone that you've spoken to Mr Gwynne?'

'Yes, that's right.'

'And he said nothing about a sale to Kenworthy's?'

'Not a word.'

'Strange.' Crouch paused. 'However, the thing may still be all in the air. All I know is that Mrs Thatcher told me that Kenworthy's intended to develop the block on which the Bird Cage stands and I understood they had already made a tentative offer. As a matter of fact, I've heard independently that Kenworthy's were opening up at Double Bay and the Bird Cage sits right in the middle of the block.'

'These women owned the building then?'

'Yes. They bought it a long time ago, when prices were very much lower. I'm surprised that Gwynne didn't know about it though.'

So was I but I didn't say so. All sorts of ideas were running through my mind but I didn't want to discuss them with Crouch.

'I think Gwynne regarded the shop, if one can call it that, as a plaything of his wife's.'

I was anxious to get away now so I thanked Crouch and left. I had things to think about. The first thing that entered my mind was that Muriel Thatcher was the governing director of Bird Cage Proprietary Limited and ran the business. If any negotiations had taken place between the Bird Cage and Kenworthy's she had most probably made them. The second thing was that if an offer had been made by Kenworthy's she had cunningly kept the fact to herself. It seemed to me unlikely she had told Isobel because if she had, Isobel would have undoubtedly told Neville. The prospect of making a fortune was surely something that a woman would find hard to keep to herself. The third and most significant point was that if Muriel took up her option on Neville's shares then she would be in a position to keep the whole of the profit from the Kenworthy sale for herself and her chosen fellow director; her husband, I was willing to bet. If that wasn't a motive for murder I had never met one.

All Muriel had to do now was to stall Kenworthy's off

until the matter of Neville's shares had been settled and there was nothing between her and a fortune. Unfortunately for my hypothetical case against the Thatchers there could be a perfectly innocent explanation of Muriel's actions. She may have told Isobel about the Kenworthy offer and Isobel had refrained from telling her husband because the negotiations had reached only a tentative stage. She could say that anyway and I had no means of disproving it. Or maybe Neville did know but decided that the matter wasn't worth mentioning to me. I had better telephone him and find out. I made the call as soon as I got back to Headquarters.

'Did you know that your wife and Mrs Thatcher were contemplating selling the Bird Cage?' I asked him, when we were connected.

'Selling it? No, I certainly did not. Where did you get that from?'

'Crouch, the company solicitor.'

'That's a damned funny thing. Isobel didn't say a word to me.'

'But would she? From what you said I gathered that she kept her business affairs very much to herself.'

'That's true but it doesn't mean she wouldn't have talked to me about an important thing like that. She wouldn't have allowed me to interfere and probably wouldn't have taken my advice but she would have certainly mentioned the matter.'

'I am inclined to think she didn't know and to my way of thinking that is an important point. You are sure she would have told you?'

'Oh yes. She told me when she and Muriel proposed to buy the building, in fact it was my back that financed the deal.'

'You told me you knew nothing about any agreement between the two women.'

'That's right.'

116

'You don't know then that under the terms of their agreement the surviving partner has first option on the other partner's shares?'

'No, but I guessed there would be some provision of that kind. I think I mentioned that.'

'Yes, you did. But the point is rather more important now. You are obliged to sell your half of the business to Mrs Thatcher.'

'That's all right with me. The Bird Cage must be worth quite a lot of money now.'

'It's going to be worth a great deal more before long. Kenworthy's are interested in the property and I have some reason to believe they may have already made a tentative offer.'

'Well it's news to me but I don't see how it affects me except to make my shares a little more valuable.'

I hung up at this point with a brief word to the effect that I hoped this future good fortune would offer some consolation for the loss of his wife. Gwynne said that nothing would do that and our conversation ended.

It had been my intention to explain to Gwynne that Mrs Thatcher stood to gain considerably from Isobel's death. Despite his obvious business experience he hadn't seen the possibility himself or couldn't believe that Mrs Thatcher would take advantage of the situation but I realized as I spoke to him that he was going to have to talk business with her and I didn't want him to give her any indication that I was interested in the matter. I was well aware that Mrs Thatcher could simply deny that Kenworthy's had made even a tentative offer. All I had was the statement from Crouch that he 'understood' that they had. If such an offer had been made it would, of course, have been made to the company, not to Mrs Thatcher personally. But she had been in a position to conceal the fact.

Naturally Kenworthy's would know whether they had made an offer or not but I knew enough about big business to realize that they would almost certainly deny having done so. Since they would want to acquire any property they needed at the lowest possible price they wouldn't encourage news of specific offers to become public, the most they would admit to would be an 'interest' in the area and they'd admit that only because of the difficulty of keeping their operations entirely secret. In all probability, if I went to see them I would be met with a bland refusal to divulge any information about what they would regard as highly confidential matters. I doubted whether I had the power at this stage to demand their co-operation. It looked to me therefore as if Mrs Thatcher was sitting very prettily indeed.

All the same I thought I had better go and see her. If she and her husband had murdered Isobel Gwynne we were going to have a lot of trouble proving it, so before tackling the problem in earnest I ought to find out whether it was possible or not.

At four o'clock I drove out to Double Bay. I wasn't at all sure how I was going to handle Mrs Thatcher but I decided to take a good look at her first and then make up my mind. I intended to find out first whether she and her husband had an alibi for Saturday night and if they hadn't I might pop in some awkward questions about the Bird Cage.

Many years ago Double Bay had been just another pleasant harbourside suburb but for some reason it had attracted many European migrants who had been largely instrumental in turning it into a smart, cosmopolitan area with some expensive restaurants and elegant shops. The Bird Cage was one of the latter, though its appeal was clearly directed to the teenager in-group. One entered through a large, highly decorative, white-painted framework shaped like a bird cage and encouraged on one's way by muted pop music, piped through the premises. But it was the birds inside the cage that caught my masculine eye.

By birds I mean the shop assistants though the term was far too prosaic a name for these delightful creatures. Each was dressed from head to foot in a single bright colour, a different one for each girl. The one who approached me wore canary yellow. Starting from her feet, she had on canary yellow shoes, stockings, a tunic-like dress in the same colour with a very short, flared mini-skirt and a canary yellow bow on her blonde hair. Over her left breast was a tiny bird cage design embroidered in black silk. I noticed other girls in vermilion, turquoise, green and orange.

The shop extended to the rear of the building, each separate section being divided by psychedelic gadgetry. Stairs led to departments above. A large number of customers, all women, gave the place a busy air. My canary yellow bird smiled at me and asked what she could do for me. I thought of a number of things because, like all the girls I had seen, she was very attractive. Someone, presumably Muriel Thatcher, had a highly developed skill in presentation. I told Canary Yellow that I wished to speak to Mrs Thatcher and wondered at the same time whether she would be wearing the uniform and what colour she had chosen.

Canary Yellow looked a bit doubtful and when I said I was Detective Sergeant Gray of the C.I.B. she looked even more doubtful.

'Tell Mrs Thatcher,' I said pleasantly, 'that I want to see her in connection with the death of Mrs Gwynne.'

'Oh.'

Canary Yellow looked sad but trotted off quickly, a flick of her canary yellow skirt revealing for a brief instant some enticing canary yellow curves. The girls wore tights. I waited, filling in the time by watching Turquoise a redhead, and Vermilion a brunette and then Canary Yellow came back and escorted me to an office at the back of the shop.

If the Bird Cage itself shrieked 'get with it' the office whispered Harvard School of Business Administration. It was severely decorated in white and grey and looked orderly and efficient. So did Muriel Thatcher.

'Please sit down,' she said to me.

She was a dark-haired woman around forty, plainly but expensively dressed in black. She was exquisitely made up, professionally hairdressed and incredibly neat but a faint indentation in her jawline and etched lines around her eyes gave her age away. She reminded me of that curious breed of women who shove their way to the top and love nothing better than to boast about it, a smiling cosmetic surface over a steel trap. For the moment I thought my best plan was to act the dumb cop and allow her to retain her comfortable sense of superiority until some sort of picture emerged. I sat down.

'You wanted to see me about poor Isobel, I understand,' she said with some impatience as I hadn't yet said a word.

'Yes. She was your partner, wasn't she?'

'Yes.'

'Did you know her intimately?'

'No.'

I had my notebook out and wrote rather slowly. I waved my hand casually around the office.

'Who gets it now?' I asked.

'I beg your pardon?'

'Who owns the bazaar now? Is it yours?'

She stared at me coldly.

'Is that relevant?'

I raised my eyebrows.

'Don't you want to answer that?'

'I am quite prepared to answer sensible questions.'

I wrote again.

'Forget it,' I said airily. 'We'll have Mrs Gwynne's will shortly: we'll get to it then. Know Strathwood?'

'If that means do I know Strathwood country club the answer is yes, a little.'

'Mrs Gwynne was murdered there.'

'So I believe.'

'Nasty business. Of course you weren't there last week-end?'

'No, I wasn't.'

'But you have been there though?'

'Yes, once.'

'With Mr and Mrs Gwynne?'

'Yes.'

'I suppose you were at a nightclub or somewhere on Saturday?'

'I don't see that it's any business of yours.'

'Oh, we like to know where everyone was.' I paused, pen in hand. 'You don't want to tell me where you were?'

'Not unless you can give me a good reason for asking.'

'How long had you known Mrs Gwynne?'

'About six years.'

'Six years? That's quite a long time. Yet you say you didn't know her well.'

'We were just business partners.'

'Oh? You went with the Gwynnes to Strathwood on business then?'

She could have spat at me.

'That was social.'

'You knew Mrs Gwynne socially then? As well as through your business partnership?'

'A little.'

'But not intimately?'

'That's what I said.'

'So you did. You knew she was going to Strathwood last week-end?'

'She went there often.'

'You knew she went there often?'

'I've just said so.'

'Then you knew she was going there last week-end? Or did you know she was going there every time she went except that particular week-end?'

She looked at me suspiciously but I maintained my bland, slightly dumb expression.

'She told me she was going there last week-end.'

'Did you know that Mr Gwynne was going to return to Sydney on Saturday night?'

'Isobel did mention it.'

'But on Saturday you were home watching TV?'

'I said nothing about watching television.'

'Everybody watches TV. And you were home? Or were you?'

'We were home.'

'Alone?'

'I don't see why you should be asking me these questions.'

'Madam,' I said, with the weary air of an underling trying to do his duty. 'I have been instructed to question everyone who knew Mrs Gwynne. Do you and Mr Thatcher own a car?'

'We have two cars,' she snapped, unable to bear the thought that even a dumb cop should think them too poor to own a car.

'You *are* lucky,' I said innocently. I looked around. 'I suppose this place is worth a few quid?'

'I don't see why that should concern you.'

'Oh, it does. I understand Kenworthy's are buying up in this district. I suppose they haven't made you an offer?'

She had been poker-faced through most of the interview, just now and then letting her guard down sufficiently to indicate that she'd like to choke me to death. Now, I thought, she was definitely on the defensive.

'What makes you ask that?'

'Oh, just information received.'

'Why should the police be interested in what Kenworthy's do? I don't understand you.'

'Ah, but then you are probably not a very good business woman. If you were you'd know that financial dealings by companies as big as Kenworthy's attract a lot of smart guys out to make a fast buck, as they say. We have a financial squad to keep an eye open for them. *Have* Kenworthy's approached you?'

I think at this point she decided that I wasn't quite as innocent as I looked as her own expression was wary. I could almost see her mind at work wondering just how much I knew of Kenworthy's activities. Perhaps she thought I might be suspicious if she claimed not to have had an offer when other owners in the block had.

'We have had an inquiry from Kenworthy's,' she admitted.

'We? You mean Mrs Gwynne knew of this ... er, inquiry?'

'Of course.'

'That's funny. Mr Gwynne knew nothing about it.'

'Perhaps Mrs Gwynne didn't tell him. It was purely an exploratory move on the part of Kenworthy's. In any case we hadn't made up our minds whether we would sell or not if we did receive an offer.'

'Have you been in touch with Mr Gwynne as the new part owner of this place?'

'It's only a couple of days since Isobel died. I thought I'd give him a chance to recover from the shock before worrying him with business matters.'

'Very kind of you. Just to refer back to the question you didn't answer. Did you have any visitors on Saturday night?'

She was suddenly angry.

'I don't like your questions,' she said sharply.

'Do you wish to make a complaint? You can see Detective Inspector Lindon; he's in charge of the case.'

'It looks very much as if you were asking me to provide

an alibi for Saturday night.'

'Mrs Thatcher. I've already asked about forty people to account for their movements on Saturday night. Obviously most if not all of them are completely innocent and therefore have nothing to worry about. If you do not wish to answer my questions please say so and I'll pass the information on to my superiors and they can then take whatever action they consider necessary.'

She pulled a wry face but decided to answer.

'We had no visitors on Saturday. I'd had a very busy week and went to bed early. My husband stayed up for a while reading and then came to bed.'

'Thank you. That's very clear. Now let me read over my notes in case I've missed something. You'll be asked to put this into a formal statement later if it is considered necessary. You've known the Gwynnes for about six years and have had some social contact with them. You have been to Strathwood once yourself and knew that the Gwynnes were going there last week-end and that Mr Gwynne would not be there on Saturday night. You and your husband spent the evening at home and had no visitors. Finally you have had an inquiry from Kenworthy's but up to the time of Mrs Gwynne's death had not made up your mind whether to sell or not. That's it, I think. Just a few more points. Do you know of anyone who harboured a grudge against Mrs Gwynne sufficiently to want to murder her?'

'I do not.'

She looked about ready to bite me.

'May I have your private address please.'

'Twenty-one Chase Road, Pymble,' she spat.

'And your husband's business address?'

'He's an accountant with Clarke and Company in George Street.'

I stood up.

'Thank you, Mrs Thatcher. I can find my own way out. Good afternoon.'

I left her staring after me venomously. In contrast Canary Yellow gave me a beaming smile as I passed through the shop. I hoped Mrs Thatcher didn't see her or Canary Yellow might have had her canary yellow bottom smacked, figuratively speaking.

I went straight from the Bird Cage to Clarke and Company knowing that Muriel Thatcher would have almost certainly telephoned her husband. He was one of the new breed of accountants, smart, watchful and on the way up. I knew he had been warned to watch his tongue because he was charming and helpful, telling the same story as his wife with a disingenuous air. Butter wouldn't have melted in his mouth but I guessed dollar notes would have melted in his pocket ... fast. He was well turned out and a trifle foppish but underneath, I suspected, ruthless enough to grab what he wanted. I didn't think that either he or his wife would have stopped at murder if the stakes were high enough and it looked as if they were.

I went back to Headquarters and told my story to Inspector Lindon who instantly pooh-poohed it.

'I grant you there could have been some hank-panky with that sale to Kenworthy's,' he conceded. 'But how the devil could that pair get hold of Mrs Gwynne at Strathwood?'

This was the flaw in my theory.

'Well, Mrs Gwynne was somewhere. Where?'

'How the dickens do I know?' said Lindon irritably. 'If I knew that I'd have the case solved.'

I forgave him for the exaggeration but answered my own question.

'She was in her cabin waiting for Scott when the Thatchers turned up.'

'All right. Prove it.'

'I might even yet,' I said obstinately. 'I can't get over the fact that that woman stood to make perhaps a hundred thousand dollars.'

'You're guessing.'

'I know. But I'd rather have what she stood to make than your superannuation.'

'Who wouldn't? But why should the Thatchers expect to find Mrs Gwynne in her cabin? Or anywhere else for that matter?'

'Look, Bob,' I said, 'I don't pretend to know all the details. But it's not impossible that they found her. They could have gone to Strathwood, timing their arrival to co-incide with Gwynne's departure. They would know when he had to leave. In any event they would have been pre-pared to wait for the chance of getting Mrs Gwynne alone. You haven't seen that pair but I have and in my opinion they would have been prepared to wait all night for a hun-dred thousand dollars. My theory is that they picked her up somewhere round seven or a bit earlier and kept her prisoner until later . . .'

'For heaven's sake why?'

'So that they could murder her at a time when the people at Strathwood could come under suspicion. I admit that at the moment I haven't got any evidence but my idea fits well. It explains why we haven't been able to discover where Mrs Gwynne was between seven and the time she was murdered, it explains why she hadn't had intercourse or anything to eat and drink. It explains why her clothes were ripped off . . .'

'Does it? Why?'

'To give the impression that some half-crazed man had been at work. It explains one of the things that has puzzled us, me at any rate, from the beginning. I mean the basic contradiction in the way she was murdered. On the one hand it looked like a carefully planned effort with pre-parations made beforehand but on the other it looked like the impulsive action of a man suddenly driven to a terrible revenge.'

Lindon laughed a little cynically.

'There's no doubt about you, Doug. You're an expert at making bricks without straw. All this is pure guesswork. What are we supposed to do? Go and arrest them now?'

This was where the old devil had me. I had no clear idea about what to do next. If the Thatchers had engineered a plot to gain control of the Bird Cage and murdered Isobel Gwynne in the process they had done it very skilfully. I didn't see how I was going to prove that they had actually gone to Strathwood unless I could find someone who saw them there and that was the key to the problem. All the same if I didn't know what to do next I didn't believe Uncle Bob knew either. And I could point a finger too.

'Obviously,' I said, 'we can't arrest the Thatchers on what we've got but we can't arrest anyone else either. What do *you* suggest we do?'

'Ah,' said the Inspector with a certain satisfaction, 'I was just about to tell you. In spite of all your fancy theories I am still convinced that someone at Strathwood murdered Mrs Gwynne. I know we're stuck for the time being on those three men we first suspected but there were other men at Strathwood, including your friend Reeves, so the hunt isn't over by a long chalk. Now what I propose to do is this. We are going to interview all the guests again and the staff as well.'

'Hell! The whole lot?'

'Yes. Everyone.'

'But they'll be all over the place.'

'I don't care. We have their addresses. I look at it this way. When we interrogated them on Sunday night we knew little about what had happened so we weren't able to ask the right questions. We know a bit more now. As well as that, some of that crowd may have been a bit careless about what they said. I haven't forgotten that mob who claimed to have gone to bed at a quarter past one but were sitting around drinking till much later. The point is, Doug, that someone may have seen or heard something and didn't think it important enough to mention so this time I want some really intensive questioning and I want statements in writing. If we don't come up with some useful facts from this effort we'll have to think about widening our field a bit and interrogating all the people on that list Alec Reeves is preparing. I'd sooner not do that, it will mean a hell of a lot of work, but we may have to.'

I accepted the situation philosophically. My part in the exercise was to do the interrogating. I could have as many men as I wanted but experience had shown me that questions were only worth asking when the questioner was thoroughly familiar with all aspects of the subject ... and that meant me. What I would do was to take a stenographer with me, record the questions and answers, bring the results back to Headquarters, have them typed up in the form of statements and send constables out to get them signed. The Inspector was to be the co-ordinator of the programme and all the statements would go to him as soon as they were ready. Thus, he claimed, he would have all the available information at his fingertips, tabulated, cross-checked, timed and recorded in detail. Admittedly Uncle Bob was good at this and would spot any gaps and discrepancies in the evidence at once. The trouble was that I thought it very unlikely we'd find any gaps and discrepancies.

Nevertheless, there was a slim chance that something would turn up to give us a new lead and for that reason the effort could be considered worthwhile. In fact from my point of view it might turn out to be a godsend as I might come across evidence that some outsiders had been around; even the sound of a car or something like that could be a pointer. Since I was going to do the interrogating I would make sure that the questions covered every possibility including the presence of the Thatchers at Strathwood.

That night I took Pat to dinner and for the time being

forgot murder except to ask her a few brief questions about Strathwood enthusiasts who happened to be absent during the recent week-end. But she wasn't able to help.

'Look, Douglas, hundreds of people have been to Strathwood since I started going there. As I've told you, Isobel was always making a play for some man or other, when Neville wasn't around of course. It's quite possible that she had a violent affair with a man without a soul knowing anything about it. From what I've read,' she smiled knowingly, 'I gather that the most torrid love affairs are the ones kept most secret.'

I groaned inwardly. If the Thatchers could have sneaked into Strathwood and murdered Isobel so could some unknown male from the murky recesses of Isobel's past. There didn't have to be a short time-limit, some besotted individual from maybe several months back could have suddenly gone berserk after nursing a real or fancied grievance until it burst. After some years in the police force I knew what stupidities some men could come to when enamoured of a particular female, often a female who failed to interest most men. I dreaded the thought of having to dig back into the past histories of several dozen men.

On Wednesday morning I began a week of travelling, talking and listening. My assistants and I covered damned nearly the whole of Sydney chasing up people who lived as far apart as Sutherland and Hornsby, not to mention a trip to Strathwood to deal with the staff. With the initial reports and the final signed statements we gathered enough material to stock a small library but for all the good it proved it might have been written in Minoan Linear B script. True we now knew, or thought we knew, what everyone had done, where they had been and who had slept with whom but we still didn't know where Isobel Gwynne had been from seven to the time she died and who had murdered her.

Uncle Bob had been growing steadily more irritated and was ready for a couple of months' holiday. So was I. I'd done all the running about.

'I don't get it, Doug,' the Inspector complained for the tenth time. 'If all this junk is to be believed the woman just vanished from the face of the earth for six hours or more. Where the devil *was* she?'

I didn't know and said so. My money was still on the Thatchers but I refrained from mentioning the fact. Lindon, I knew, would come round in his own good time but he was so angry at the failure of his plan that I felt it unwise to prod him. By this time we had Alec Reeves' list and the Inspector was making threatening noises at it. But he realized as well as I did what a marathon it would be to check it thoroughly and our lack of success with the people who had actually been at Strathwood during the fatal week-end wasn't exactly encouraging.

For a few days we did nothing but mull over the data we had collected, a process that got us nowhere. When I say we did nothing, I mean nothing in relation to the Gwynne case; as always there were dozens of minor problems to attend to and these kept us occupied while the Inspector tried to make up his mind about our next move.

In point of fact the next move turned out to be mine, not ours, and I was able to make it because of a lucky break. According to the books, the best detectives solve their cases by masterly demonstrations of induction and deduction but this is only possible when one has all the information and in practice much of it remains obstinately hidden. Actually it wasn't information I acquired but a hint about where to look for it and this came from a very unlikely source.

One night Pat Morland and I were invited to a private screening of some very old comedy films including a couple of Chaplin's very earliest. These were still excruciatingly funny despite their age and the changes in film technique and style that have occurred since they were made. Some of the tricks and devices seemed a little crude to modern eyes but one short episode stuck in my mind and set me thinking along very strange lines. The idea, once implanted, continued to grow until I became convinced that I had a possible solution to the problem of Isobel Gwynne's murder. I had to prove my case though and provide some material evidence, which was going to be extremely difficult if not impossible. As a theory it was fine but Inspector Lindon wasn't going to be impressed unless I could come up with a bloodstained fingerprint or something equally persuasive.

So I didn't discuss my notion with Lindon, I merely told him I had an idea that might lead to the discovery of Mrs Gwynne's murderer and I proposed, with his permission, to set about testing it. He growled a little when I refused to explain my plans in detail on the grounds that my theory could be madly astray but he came round when I pointed out diplomatically that if he knew nothing he couldn't be blamed for the waste of time and money if I proved to be wrong.

When I came to think about how to tackle my problem I found myself in something of a quandary. I hoped to obtain some evidence by examining Ray Mansell's car and if I found it I would establish with some certainty how Mrs Gwynne was murdered but not who murdered her, though some pointer to this might well emerge. At the same time the lack of this evidence did not necessarily prove my theory wrong, it just made it a hell of a lot more difficult to prove. There were other tests I planned to make, experiments to determine the feasibility of my ideas. My dilemma lay in deciding which to do first. Test the feasibility? Or look for the evidence? It was a waste of time looking for evidence if my idea wouldn't work and there would be a sudden death quality about failure to find it. I decided on a feasibility study, as they call it, first.

This meant a trip to Strathwood, quite an exciting trip for me because I was going to test out what Inspector Lindon would call an airy-fairy theory. In fact if he knew what I was going to do he would probably use stronger language than that. I took two men with me, a constable of normal build, which meant one of around twelve and a half stone and the lightest probationary constable I could find, a mere nineteen-year-old stripling weighing something under eleven. I also took with me the original chair and the wooden box that had been used in Isobel Gwynne's murder.

The store shed had been kept locked since my last visit to Strathwood but I had the key and opened up the place for a quick check to see if all I needed was there. It was and the constables and I spent a happy half-hour carrying out numerous experiments which, to my intense gratification, were completely successful. Now for the evidence.

I knew I was going to have to be very lucky indeed to find this but I had to try. It would have been frustrating to the nth degree to have concocted a beautiful theory, to have proved its feasibility and then to have it disbelieved for the want of some piece of solid matter I could lay in front of Inspector Lindon. I drove back to town, sent my assistants on to Headquarters with instructions not to speak of our morning's work to anyone, and went to see Ray Mansell. I expected to have a sticky half-hour with him and got it. I wanted to examine his car but I didn't want to tell him why so I had to do a lot of fast talking to explain to him that neither he nor his wife was in any way involved but that the murderer had made use of the fact that Mansell's car had been parked immediately in front of the store shed that Saturday night. A little reluctantly he took me down to the parking basement and unbent to the extent of lending me a torch so that I could crawl under the car's front end and search for what I wanted.

I shall never forget the solid satisfaction I felt when I

found it. It was an achievement, I thought. A theory vindicated. Mansell looked mystified as I wrapped the precious bit of evidence in a handkerchief but I told him he would no doubt know what it meant at some later date. I hurried back to Headquarters.

To my relief, Uncle Bob was in. I wasted no time but told him that I knew how Isobel Gwynne was killed. He just gaped.

'What are you talking about, Doug?' he demanded. 'We know how she was killed.'

'Do we?'

'Of course we do. She was strung up on that rafter and the chair pulled from under her.'

'By whom?'

'For heaven's sake, by the murderer, of course. Who else?'

I shook my head.

'The murderer was nowhere near the shed when that chair was pulled away.'

Lindon looked at me as if I had suddenly gone round the bend. I could almost see the words airy-fairy forming in his mind and sure enough out they came.

'Is this another one of your airy-fairy theories?'

'It's more than a theory . . . I have some proof.'

The Inspector watched me with a look of frowning disbelief as I took out my handkerchief and unwrapped a piece of binder twine. It was about two feet long, frayed at the ends and blackened with grease for several inches in the centre. I laid it carefully on Lindon's desk.

'What the devil's that?' he demanded.

'It's a piece of binder twine. I've just removed it from the underside of Mr Mansell's car.'

Lindon shook his head.

'Now look, Doug, I'm busy . . .'

'Hold your horses, Bob. This is important. Mrs Gwynne was killed when the murderer was miles away and I think I know how he did it.'

'All right. Let's have it.'

'Can I tell the story in my own way ... from the beginning?'

'O.K. I'll listen. But it had better be good.'

Lindon sat back and began to fill his pipe. I started to
speak.

'Well, I think this murder was the result of careful prep-
aration. Some time on that Saturday afternoon the murderer slipped into the store shed and got everything ready.
He didn't have to do much, just find a suitable box and a
chair and place them in a handy position and find a leather
strap long enough to serve his purpose. No doubt he broke
off a few lengths of twine and put them where he
could find them easily too. The piece of rag he later used as
a gag probably went into his pocket as he would need to use
it somewhere outside the shed. Remember he was going to
have to work in a fairly dim light and he would need to lay
his hands on his bits and pieces without too much delay. I
don't know where Mrs Gwynne was when the murderer
grabbed her but it was probably on the car park soon after
Neville Gwynne left and that isn't too far from the store
shed. At any rate, I suggest that he caught her unawares
and shoved the gag on her before she had a chance to cry
out. He could then carry her across to the shed in reasonable safety. No doubt she struggled like mad but she wasn't
very big and an ordinary man could have managed her
without difficulty. Once inside the shed he could take
things a little more quietly and tie her up without hurrying.
We know what he did next. He put her on the chair,
climbed up on the box beside her and strung her from the
rafter with the leather strap.'

The Inspector was looking at me dolefully but he didn't
say anything. I ploughed on.

'The next bit is the really important bit. At this point he
had her standing on the chair, just balanced, with the strap

fairly taut and her clothes ripped down to her ankles. The murderer intended her to stay like that until after the party and the Mansells' car was driven away. Remember it was parked just outside the store shed just a few feet from the door . . .'

'What the devil did the Mansells' car have to do with it?'

'I'm coming to that. The murderer took a length of twine, maybe fifteen feet or more, and looped it round one of the front legs of the chair. Then he carried it out to Mansell's car, passing it under the store shed door, and looped it round the front axle, tying the ends together so that he had, in effect, a continuous loop from the car to the chair. You can see what that meant. When Mansell backed his car away about one-fifteen, he pulled the twine and jerked the chair from under Isobel Gwynne and she died.'

'Hell, Doug, would that work?'

'It did work. I'm certain of it. This morning I took Jack Luscombe with me to Strathwood. He doesn't weigh much more than about ten and a half stone and it worked with him so it must have worked with Mrs Gwynne. We didn't put the strap round his neck of course but under his armpits but it held him and when we linked the chair to the police car and backed it away, Jack was left dangling. I got Constable Smithers to back the car while I stayed inside and watched. It worked perfectly.'

Lindon shook his head unbelievingly.

'I don't get it. Wouldn't that twine break?'

'No, it's quite strong. You can't break it with your hands unless you use the old shop assistant's trick and snap it against itself and even then it doesn't break easily. But in any case, it didn't need to be all that strong. You see Isobel Gwynne was balanced in an upright position on a chair that was firm enough to take her weight yet a bit wobbly. The slightest movement of the chair and she would lose her balance and transfer her weight to the strap. No doubt when the pull came on the twine she did lose her balance and all the twine had to do was to pull the chair from under her kicking legs. Naturally the loop of twine came off the chair leg and was carried away by Mansell's car.'

'You sure you're right about this, Doug? Wouldn't Mansell have become suspicious finding a length of string attached to his car?'

'The chance that he'd find it was remote. It was looped round his front axle, well underneath the front end. He wouldn't have discovered it before he drove off from in front of the store shed because both he and his wife approached the car from the rear. They had no reason to go to the front of the car. Then when they drove off the twine was dragged along the ground under the car. My guess is that after three or four miles over gravel roads to their farm the twine wore through. I took a chance that a bit of it remained tangled round the brake rods or something and I was lucky. That bit was caught against a shock absorber, gummed in place with oil and grease. I'm willing to bet a month's salary that if we analyse it we'll find that it's the same stuff that the murderer used to tie up Mrs Gwynne.'

'You've got an answer for everything, haven't you? How the devil did you manage to tumble to this?'

I grinned.

'It's an odd sort of story. I happened to see some very old Chaplin films the other night and an incident in one of them gave me the idea. Chaplin was at a very smart party and some haughty wench was being very rude to him so he decided to take her down a peg or two. He used a very old trick. He waited until she was about to sit down and then walked behind the chair and hooked it away with the crook of his cane. Of course she landed on her backside with her legs up in the air. Actually she didn't show much more than a modern girl does when she sits down but I guess when the film was made it was horribly embarrassing for a girl to show her drawers to an assembled crowd. The visual picture of that chair being moved stayed in my mind and I began to wonder whether the murderer hadn't used some device to drag the chair from under Isobel when he was miles away.'

The Inspector relit his pipe and stared at me through a cloud of smoke.

'It's a damned ingenious idea and I must say that you were pretty smart to have worked it out but where does it get us?'

'Well, it explains why we haven't been able to find any traces of Mrs Gwynne between seven o'clock and when she died.'

'That unfortunate woman stood on that chair for about six hours? It's a wonder she didn't collapse.'

'Human beings are highly resilient when it comes to matters of life and death but it wouldn't have mattered if she *had* collapsed. If she'd fainted or lost her balance she would have strangled herself and died earlier but Mansell's car would have pulled the chair away and toppled it just the same. The only difference is that we would have been looking for a murderer who operated at ten or eleven instead of at half past one.'

'Maybe, but what murderer?'

'We have two prime suspects now.'

'Two?'

'Yes. Scott and Reeves.'

'Ah, yes. Reeves again. The set-up was perfect for him, he knew that shed better than anyone. But what about Gwynne? Doesn't he come into the picture now?'

I shook my head.

'He wouldn't have had time. He was at the Wentworth with his client by nine-fifteen so he must have met the eight-thirty plane from Melbourne. If he left Strathwood around ten to seven he must have only just made it. He certainly couldn't have left any later. As it was he must have driven pretty fast.'

'This shop woman you were so keen about. Could she and her husband have picked up Mrs Gwynne just before seven and taken her to the store shed?'

'Theoretically, yes. Depends on whether they knew that a car was going to be parked outside the store shed. Since they had stayed at Strathwood they could have known that so they're suspects all right. In their case it wouldn't have been necessary to make prior preparations as they would have had plenty of time once they'd got Mrs Gwynne into the shed.'

'So we've still got Scott, Reeves and the Thatchers?'

I nodded.

'So we're not much better off, Doug.'

I was beginning to think that myself, which was disappointing after what I thought was a brilliant piece of detection.

'I don't know,' I said hopefully. 'We can now concentrate our attention on the early part of the evening. Scott seems our best bet since we know he was hanging about around seven. Reeves is a possible but we can check his movements. He was in sight of dozens of people most of the time.'

'It looks like another lot of interviews though I'm damned if I can see what we can do about Scott. If he or anyone else worked that trick it's going to be damned difficult to prove it.'

7

I KNEW it was going to be difficult. All detection is difficult. If it wasn't there wouldn't be any need for trained detectives. Even Commissioners could solve cases. But the difficulty I faced now was the same old difficulty: how to link a suspect with a particular place at a particular time. The Thatchers now. I was loathe to let them go because of their handsome motive and my strong feeling that Muriel was playing a shrewd game with the Bird Cage finances but none of the mass of information we had acquired from the guests at Strathwood even mentioned them so if they had been there they certainly hadn't been seen. Now that the pattern of events, according to my new theory, had shifted to the early part of the evening I might find someone who had heard their car, or one of their *two* cars, leave their home at say around six o'clock but that just wasn't good enough. Mrs Thatcher would say without a qualm that she went out to buy cigarettes and there was nothing I could do to disprove it. To be effective my evidence had to place them beyond any doubt at Strathwood.

Much the same argument applied to Scott even though he had admitted being on the spot at the relevant time. Somehow I had to prove that he actually came into contact with Isobel Gwynne. But I was puzzled about Alec Reeves. I was inclined to dismiss him as a suspect because the trick employed to murder Isobel wouldn't have helped him; he wasn't miles away when she died but right there at Strathwood. On the other hand he could have employed the trick deliberately to suggest that the murderer was someone who would have gained from it. He was quite capable of conceiving such a double bluff.

On the whole my best bet seemed to be Scott but what I could do about him I just didn't know. There didn't seem to be any point in questioning him again, all he had to do to be safe was to stick to his story.

However, once again fate stepped in, as they say. A couple of days later it happened to be Pat Morland's birthday and by way of celebration I took her to dinner at the Clarendon. The Clarendon was one of Sydney's best restaurants, hideously expensive for a Sergeant of Police but with a reputation going back to long before the new, smart, gimmick places began to spring up everywhere. The food, as expected, was excellent, so were the wines; and the conversation absolutely scintillating. We thought so anyway. But right at the end of the meal, just when I was lighting a cigarette for Pat I saw Neville Gwynne. He was in a dinner jacket and I noted with some surprise that with him was Muriel Thatcher. They were on their way out and couldn't have seen Pat and me without turning completely round. I didn't believe they had seen us earlier since we were tucked into a secluded corner of the restaurant. I cautioned Pat.

'Look round carefully, Pat,' I said. 'There's Neville Gwynne with Muriel Thatcher. Just going out.'

Pat turned her head slowly, took a quick glimpse and then faced me again.

'I wonder what they are up to?' she said. 'I didn't think Neville knew her that well.'

'Neither did I. He gave me the impression he had practically nothing to do with the Thatchers and Mrs Thatcher told me the same thing.'

'They were at Strathwood together once, you know.'

'Yes, but I gather the week-end wasn't a great success and it was their only social venture together.'

'Maybe it's just business. Neville would have to talk to Muriel now that he owns a part of the Bird Cage.'

'Business? At night? In evening dress? Muriel's dolled up too so they must be going to some social spree together. It seems a bit odd when Isobel's only been dead a couple of weeks. And where is Thatcher?'

'But, Douglas, there's nothing clandestine about their being together, they're quite open about it. Perhaps they're meeting Brian Thatcher later.'

'It could be. But the way Gwynne took her arm just now and the way they were talking to one another suggests they've been friendly for a long time. Which means that they both lied to me, by implication at any rate. I'm wondering why.'

'You don't think they've been hatching up some sort of plot together, do you?'

'I could believe anything of that woman. But as a matter of fact there's more in this than meets the eye. I can't give you the details but it's quite possible that there's some funny business going on with the Bird Cage finance. That's why I find their lying highly intriguing. They definitely claimed they didn't know one another well. I wonder where they are off to?'

'The theatre? The ballet, perhaps. It's a first night.'

'Good Lord, I wonder. You could be right you know. The theatre's right next door and they left just at the right time. It's ten to eight now.'

'It's a social event, just the sort of thing Muriel would want to be seen at. There's a new Australian ballet *The Day the Rain Came*. The papers have been making quite a fuss about it.'

'Yes, I know. Would you like to see it?'

Pat looked surprised.

'What do you mean, Douglas?'

'Well, how about going?'

'Good heavens, Douglas. It's a first night. We'd never get in.'

'I'm not so sure about that. We could pick up a cancellation. The back of the balcony would do us in the circumstances.'

Pat frowned.

'What circumstances?'

'I want to keep an eye on Gwynne.'

'But why, Douglas? He couldn't have murdered Isobel.'

'I know. But Muriel and her husband could. Gwynne might be being played for a sucker. Anyway he wasn't honest with me, I'm certain, and I want to know why. Maybe he has been having an affair with Muriel and didn't want it known.'

'Then why are they so open about it now?'

'I don't know, Pat. There are all sorts of possibilities. You'd like to see the ballet, wouldn't you?'

'I'd love to but . . .'

'Stop being difficult. If we can't get in that's the end of it but we may as well try.'

Pat smiled.

'You're mad, Douglas. We won't get in and if we did you'd never find Neville in all that crowd.'

'Let's go and see shall we?'

It wasn't altogether luck that enabled me to get the theatre seats we needed. At least I preferred to believe that it was through an intelligent appreciation of the situation. The programme was an all-Australian one and I had a strong feeling that it wasn't going to be as well supported as the Theatre Trust hoped without the backing of one of the popular traditional ballets. Of course the first-nighters would be there in force but they would come to be seen not to see the ballet and their preference would be for the front stalls. The true balletomanes would come when the seats were cheaper and the new ballet had proved itself.

We were in the theatre too late to do anything about spotting Gwynne and Muriel Thatcher before the performance and I just had to hope Pat's guess was right. At interval time I left Pat at the balcony level and slipped downstairs for a quick reconnaissance. I was lucky enough to catch a glimpse of Gwynne and watched for a second or two as Muriel joined him. If that pair hadn't been as thick as thieves for a good long time, I was willing to eat my uniform cap next time I was supposed to wear it. Men and women don't look at one another in that cosy fashion unless they've been fairly intimate and fairly, I thought, was almost certainly an understatement.

'You were right,' I told Pat when I returned to her. 'They're downstairs. I shall award you the Police Medal.'

'Thanks. You're too generous. What are you going to do after the show? Try and follow them?'

'We'll cross that bridge when we come to it. Perhaps our luck will hold.'

In fact I intended to follow Gwynne if I could but I wasn't quite sure how Pat would take to spending the last hours of her birthday chasing suspects. I thought now that Gwynne had been carrying on with Muriel Thatcher for some time and that made nonsense of his guff about seeing nothing but innocent play in his late wife's escapades. What this meant, I wasn't sure. It could be that Isobel's murder was a combined effort between Gwynne and Muriel. Though I was certain that Gwynne couldn't have had time to complete the task of hanging Isobel before driving to Sydney he might just have been able to grab her, tie her up and gag her and leave her lying on the store shed floor for Muriel to deal with later. That seemed a tough assignment for a woman but Muriel was tough. A little bigger than Isobel, she had a muscular wiry frame and any amount of determination. She could have managed it. And the stripping off of Isobel's clothes fitted nicely into the picture. I could imagine that hatchet-faced dame tearing off each garment one by one and leaving with an air of triumph at the defeat of a rival.

With the rest of the audience Pat and I went back into the theatre. Maybe I wasn't in the mood but I didn't much care for *The Day the Rain Came*. The first part was intended to convey the fierce heat of a drought in the inland with listless aborigines dancing in slow motion. Following this was the ceremonial rain-making dance, the dancers moving with increasing speed and agility to a weird mixture of Schoenberg, Wagner and snippets from Beethoven's Sixth till finally the rain fell, presumably, in a riot of frenzied abandonment. Having been born in the country and spent my early years on a farm I knew the feeling of relief and thankfulness when the rain came after a prolonged searing drought. The acrobatic cavorting of the dancers when the rain-making proved successful appeared to me to be a caricature of the aborigines' dignified acceptance of natural phenomena. Pat wasn't enthusiastic about the ballet and as soon as it was over we hurried downstairs to take up a position where we might see Gwynne and his lady friend without being seen ourselves.

Actually this part of my plan, if it could be called a plan, was a sheer gamble. I had no idea where Gwynne intended to go next, whether he had a car handy or was using taxis. My own car was parked fairly near the theatre as, being a policeman, I could take certain liberties with the parking regulations but Gwynne would have found it difficult to leave his anywhere near. I could only trust to luck. It must have been my lucky night because within a minute I saw Gwynne threading his way between the fur capes and the black ties with Muriel in tow. They passed through the foyer, emerged on the Castlereagh Street and began to walk towards Circular Quay. I grabbed Pat's hand.

'Come on, we'll follow a few yards behind them,' I said.

'But why, Douglas? What do you hope to see?'

'I don't know but I want to see it. Where's your sense of adventure?'

'I left it at home. I wouldn't mind a cup of coffee.'

'We'll have one later.'

Actually we didn't have to walk very far. Within a couple of hundred yards I played a hunch and guessed that

Gwynne was taking Muriel to the Wentworth and had his car parked there too. I stopped.

'We'll go back for the car,' I said. 'I'm pretty sure he's going to the Wentworth.'

Pat had given up arguing and turned back with a resigned air. We hurried, picked up the car and drove it to the Wentworth car park underneath the hotel. I took a look around and saw what I hoped was Gwynne's Jaguar. It was green anyway. I confirmed this by going to the parking attendant and exhibiting my warrant card.

'I'm interested in that green Jaguar,' I told him. 'I think it belongs to a Mr Neville Gwynne.'

The attendant checked his list.

'That's right. What is it? Stolen or something?'

'No. I just want to follow it out when it leaves. Nothing to do with the hotel.'

'O.K., mate.'

I went and sat in my car with Pat. She wasn't very happy.

'That pair are probably gorging themselves with food and drink while we sit around waiting,' she complained.

'We haven't any alternative but to wait. But be patient. When this is over I'll take you to my flat and give you a beautiful cup of coffee and an even more beautiful brandy. I might even make you a Café Royal if you're good.'

'A Café Royal? What's that?'

'You heat the brandy, set light to it and pour it over the coffee. It's very pleasant. Warms the cockles and all that.'

We waited a little over half an hour. Then Gwynne and Muriel Thatcher came down and we watched them get into Gwynne's car and drive off. We followed. They drove to Point Piper.

'Gwynne's place,' I said. 'What next I wonder?'

I stopped some distance away as Gwynne drove under the block of flats then I left my car, telling Pat to stay put. I moved forward cautiously and saw my quarry get into the lift in the parking area. I went back to Pat.

'I don't know where Thatcher is but that pair have gone up to the Gwynnes' flat. My guess is that they will be there some time.'

'How naughty of them. What are you going to do now? Creep in and catch them in bed?'

I grinned.

'That *would* create a stir. No, we can go home now. Sleuthing's over.'

We went to my flat. I made coffee. I put some brandy in a small silver cup I'd won at golf and put a match to it. It was good brandy and lit without being heated first. I poured it into the coffee. It floated on the coffee and burnt with a delicate blue flame. Pat was delighted.

'You're a funny sort of policeman, Douglas,' she said. 'How do you afford all this?' She looked round at my comfortable little flat.

'My brother and I share a farm. He does all the work and I collect the income . . . some of it anyway.'

'Who taught you to make Café Royals?'

'It's part of my misspent youth. Some waiter or other showed me.'

We didn't talk about the Gwynne case any more. Pat was a little browned off about it and in any case we had more interesting things to do. But I made up my mind to have another cosy little chat with Muriel Thatcher and possibly her boyfriend too.

I went to the Bird Cage at nine-thirty the next morning, a Tuesday. This time as I walked into the shop Muriel Thatcher was directing the display of some new stock. Canary Yellow was in evidence and gave me a nice smile as I passed her. This apparently didn't please dear Muriel very much because as I approached her she positively scowled at me. I decided I'd be a bit tougher this time.

'I have a few more questions to ask you, Mrs Thatcher,'

I said to her bluntly.

She took a quick glance round the shop. There were no customers at this early hour but Vermilion and Turquoise Blue were looking on in a highly interested way.

'Get those dresses on to hangers,' she said sharply and then to me: 'This way.'

She marched into her office leaving me to follow. She sat down and immediately took out a cigarette and lighted it.

'What is it this time?' she spat.

'Your relations with the Gwynnes, particularly Mr Gwynne,' I said.

'What about them?'

'You weren't quite honest with me last time I spoke to you. You claimed to have had only a formal association with Mr and Mrs Gwynne but last night you spent a considerable time in Mr Gwynne's company.'

She bridled.

'Are you having me watched?' she said angrily.

'Not you, specifically.'

This stopped her because she made the natural inference that I was having Gwynne watched. Her look became noticeably less angry and much more cautious.

'I had business to discuss with Mr Gwynne,' she said.

'I must say you do business in a pleasant way. The Clarendon, the ballet and the Wentworth.'

'It's no concern of yours how I do business.'

'On the contrary, it might well be.'

'I had tickets for the ballet. My husband is away and I didn't want to waste them.'

'I see. So after the Wentworth you went to Mr Gwynne's flat to talk business?'

'You can keep your nasty insinuations to yourself.'

Her voice, I noticed, had roughened and reverted to its natural coarseness.

'I made no insinuations. I am stating flatly that you went

to Mr Gwynne's flat late last night. Yet you gave me to understand that you had virtually no contact with the Gwynnes apart from your business association.'

'You drew the inference.'

'It's my function to draw inferences but having made them I'd now like some straight answers. If you don't wish to give them I can arrange for you to be interrogated at Headquarters later. I am asking you now whether you have been an intimate friend of Mr Gwynne's for some time or whether, as you told me before, your relationship has been strictly formal.'

'Why don't you ask him?'

'I intend to but I'd like your answer first, please.'

Up to this point I was sure that Muriel Thatcher regarded me as an inquisitive cop making a confounded nuisance of himself. This could have been true whether she was a murderess or merely a shrewd business woman out to make a small fortune from a smart deal. But she was a little worried now and her hard face showed it.

'We have been friends,' she admitted reluctantly.

'Then why did you try to persuade me that you had little or no contact with the Gwynnes outside business?'

'I didn't want to be mixed up in Isobel's death.'

'Why not?'

'It . . . it's bad for business.'

'Mrs Thatcher. Don't you realize that murder is a serious matter? Lying in such circumstances comes very close to obstructing the police in the execution of their duties.'

She didn't answer but she was far from the arrogant spitfire she'd been a few minutes before.

'What sort of relationship did the Gwynnes have with each other?' I asked her.

Relief showed in her voice now that the subject had been changed.

'Oh, the usual one for a married couple.'

'Not very satisfactory then?'

'Isobel was impossible.'

'In what way?'

She looked surprised.

'Don't tell me nobody's told you.'

'Told me what?' I asked patiently.

'She was a nymphomaniac.'

'Really? How do you know that?'

'Mr Gwynne told me, of course. Anyway I saw the way she crawled to the men at Strathwood.'

'Did you see any evidence of that here?'

'I wouldn't have allowed that sort of thing in my shop.'

'*Your* shop?'

'I ran it. Isobel was only a passenger.'

'If it's true what you say, Mrs Gwynne's conduct must have been very distressing to Mr Gwynne.'

'It was. Very.'

'He didn't consider divorcing her?'

She froze.

'I know nothing about that.'

'I see. Now since you were friendly, as you put it, with Mr Gwynne, I suppose you discussed business with him? This business I mean.'

'A little.'

'Did he know about a probable offer from Kenworthy's?'

'It wasn't probable. It was all in the air.'

'But did you tell him about it?'

'I discussed it with Isobel.'

'But did you discuss it with him?'

'I can't remember.'

'You can't remember?'

'Listen. I talked to Isobel about it and I suppose she told Neville. I can't recall whether I actually discussed it with him or not. What does it matter anyway?'

'Mr Gwynne claims he knew nothing about it.'

She answered impatiently.

'How should I know what he told Isobel?'

'Mrs Thatcher. You don't seem to realize the serious-
ness of your position. As I understand it you stand to gain
considerably from Mrs Gwynne's death. You might in fact
acquire sole control of this business.'

'How the devil did you find that out?' she said
sharply.

'Never mind how I found it out. Under the terms of
your agreement with Isobel Gwynne you . . .'

'Who told you about my agreement with Isobel?' she
said angrily. 'Did Neville?'

'It's of no importance who told me. The point is that
since you stand to gain from Mrs Gwynne's death I am
obliged to consider the possibility that you had a hand in
her murder.'

'I had nothing to do with her murder.'

'You told me before that you and your husband were
home alone all that Saturday evening. Do you wish to
amend that statement?'

'Of course I don't. We were home.'

'You were home between say half past five and half past
eight?'

She stared, her eyes wide.

'But I thought . . .'

'What did you think?'

'Didn't Isobel die late at night?'

'I am asking you where you were between half past five
and half past eight. Were you home then?'

She answered reluctantly.

'No.'

'Where were you then?'

'We drove out to Newport. We thought we might have
dinner in the hotel there after some drinks in the beer
garden.'

'Well, did you?'

'We did have a few drinks but the place was so crowded and so noisy that we came back and had dinner at home.'

'What time did you leave your house and what time did you return?'

'We left just before six and got home ... well, it was a bit after eight, I suppose.'

'Did you see anyone you knew?'

'No.'

'You were in the Newport Hotel beer garden from about half past six to half past seven?'

'Not as long as that. It was slow driving on the Saturday.'

I stood up.

'I shall probably make an attempt to check your presence in the Newport Hotel beer garden but I shall need a photograph of you and your husband to do that. Have you one here by any chance?'

'No. Not here. We have at home though.'

'Then I may call on you later. And I shall have to ask you and your husband to make formal statements. I'll be in touch. Good morning.'

Mrs Thatcher looked a much less confident female as I left her.

Canary Yellow smiled at me as I passed through the shop. I smiled back a little absent-mindedly. I had so much to think about that I went and sat in my car for a while before driving back to Headquarters.

My car was parked in a pleasant little tree-lined side street off New South Head Road but I didn't pay much attention to the scene. My mind was on Neville Gwynne. Muriel Thatcher had been extremely revealing. It was now clear that Gwynne had known all along about his wife's infidelities and that made him a complete liar. The question was why had he lied? The obvious answer was because he had murdered her and his claimed ignorance of her misbehaviour successfully hid his motive. There could be no question about the latter; he knew what she had been doing and had taken his revenge. Or at least that was what seemed possible. The angry tearing of the clothes from her still-living body fitted neatly into a revenge theory. Though this could have been the work of a vicious woman like Muriel Thatcher or of a jealous male like Duncan Scott a more rational explanation was that the complete exposure of her naked body was a device employed by an angry husband to demonstrate what a promiscuous bitch his wife had been.

But if Gwynne had killed his wife how had he managed to do it? I couldn't believe he could have carried out all he had to do in much less than fifteen minutes. Gagging her, carrying her to the store shed, tying her wrists and ankles, attaching the strap to the rafter, looping it around her neck. stripping her garment by garment and finally arranging the twine to connect the chair with the Mansells' car. Tying her wrists and ankles alone could have taken several minutes because it was very unlikely that she had submitted without some sort of struggle. In fact a cautious murderer would have allowed considerable time for this as she could have fought like a wildcat, knowing that once she was bound she was completely at his mercy.

Fifteen minutes off the time Gwynne took to drive to Mascot just wasn't possible. Even on his schedule as we knew it he would have had to drive pretty fast. The alternative? I had already considered that Gwynne's task was merely to immobilize Isobel so that Muriel could later finish the job. But that meant that Brian Thatcher was also in the plot since he was with his wife during the early part of the evening. I didn't fancy the idea of a threesome though it wasn't entirely out of the question. All of them stood to gain. And the Thatchers' alibi at Newport wasn't worth a cent. On a Saturday afternoon the hotel would have been busy with hundreds of people who had been sailing on Pittwater or surfing on the beach. It was a very large place with an extensive beer garden served by dozens of waiters. The possibility that one of them could identify the Thatchers, even from a photograph, was remote. No doubt many of them were temporary staff employed to deal with the Saturday afternoon rush. So the Thatchers *could* have been at Strathwood.

One thing I felt sure of. I was getting close to the heart of the puzzle. Gwynne had lied like a trooper, Muriel Thatcher had lied like a trooper; neither had lied for nothing, I was willing to bet. But perhaps it had been an all-Thatcher job and Gwynne merely a tool. Muriel may have persuaded him to keep quiet about his wife's pecca-dilloes on the grounds that it wasn't a very nice thing to have bruited abroad. The Thatchers could have arrived at Strathwood just before Gwynne left. If they'd known when Gwynne was to meet his client at Mascot they could have worked out what time he had to leave Strathwood and planned their arrival accordingly. Two of them together would have had no difficulty in handling Isobel and once they had her in the store shed the rest would have been easy. Pymble to Strathwood was only forty-five minutes fast driving so they would have had plenty of time if they had left home at five-forty-five and even allowing half an hour for waiting about and then placing a bound and gagged Isobel in her final position they could have been home soon after eight.

Of course they would have run some risks. They prob-ably weren't sufficiently familiar with Strathwood to be certain that no one would want to visit the store shed before Isobel died. Or was that a carefully calculated risk? Saturday night was party night and I imagined that even the staff would relax after the dinner dishes had been done and other domestic details attended to. It was highly un-likely that anyone would go to the store shed at such a time. All the same, somebody took that risk.

At this stage in my reasoning I had a certain misgiving. I had to be careful not to allow my ideas to run away with me. Muriel Thatcher's prevarications may have been due solely to her financial plotting; maybe she could be convicted of opportunism not murder. This was brought home to me by consideration of the fact that, of all people, Alec Reeves was best equipped to assess the risk of Isobel being found before she was dead. Much as I disliked the idea I had still to regard him as a possible suspect. Scott too. Even he would have known better than the Thatchers how likely it was that someone would visit the store shed on a Saturday night.

What should I do next then? Check Mrs Thatcher's story against her husband's? This, I knew, was a waste of time but in accordance with established practice it had to be done. A thousand to one Mrs Thatcher would have telephoned her husband and their stories would match. Tackle Gwynne next? I decided against it. Unless I could find some crack in his alibi, and that seemed impossible, I would be wasting my time there too.

I supposed I ought to find out just where Alec Reeves was around seven o'clock. This would at least relieve my mind and satisfy Inspector Lindon, who was somewhat suspicious of Reeves. It meant a trip to Strathwood to interview the staff again but that was unavoidable and might even be useful. A fresh look at the scene might spark off a few new ideas.

I started the car and drove into town to see Brian Thatcher. As expected, it proved to be a waste of time; he had his story off pat and it duplicated his wife's. I left him with my suspicions intact. The alleged visit to the Newport Hotel seemed to me to be phoney. Both the Thatchers were socially conscious I was prepared to bet and they would have known before they set out that the Newport pub, plumb in the middle of a Sydney holiday resort, would be crowded with a great mob of surfers, surfies, yachtsmen, Saturday afternoon beer drinkers and other sports-men. No one in his right mind would go there for a quiet drink, not on a Saturday.

As it was still only twenty past ten I decided to go out to Strathwood right away and try to clear up the question of Alec's movements. I wasn't keen on the task. Alec, I be-lieved, was a good employer and I might find some resist-ance on the part of his staff to answering questions that appeared to incriminate him. But I had to admit that In-spector Lindon had some weighty reasons for suspecting Alec and these had to be answered.

According to my recollection Alec was in the dining-room for dinner that Saturday and left it a little after the Gwynnes departed. He must have gone to the office then because Duncan Scott would have gone there in order to tell Alec he was leaving and to pay his bill. The question was where did Alec go then? He didn't remain in the office because Pat and I passed through the hall shortly after-wards on our way to the lounge and the office was closed. Alec kept the office locked in his absence because it con-tained money and his various books and papers but while he was inside the door was always open. He therefore went to his bedroom, to the kitchen area or out to the car park since he didn't appear in the lounge until later. If he went to the car park he must have gone there immediately after Scott but if Scott was telling the truth then Alec was in the clear since if Scott failed to find Isobel, Alec did also.

Isobel must have been taken to the store shed between the time her husband left and the time Scott reached the car park. I didn't know exactly how long a period that was and I had no prospect of finding out since people didn't conduct their lives by stop watch. It could have been as long as ten minutes though equally it might have been only two or three but an agile, athletic type like Alec could have got hold of Isobel, clapped a hand over her mouth and had her helpless in the store shed in ten or twenty seconds.

Scott, after he had paid his bill, may have gone to his room to pick up his bag. Alec might well have known this as Scott's room was in the main building. Alec may have slipped out via the back door, whipped Isobel into the store shed and tied her up and that was where she could have been when Scott turned up on the car park to look for her.

I didn't much like the direction my thoughts were taking. Alec need not have been very long in the store shed. All he had to do was to secure Isobel and leave her lying on the floor. I had an awkward thought. Alec, to be on the safe side, could have locked the door. *Only he had the key.* A second visit to the store shed to complete his task could have been made at any time during the evening. With all the drinking and dancing and coming and going associated with the party no one would have noticed Alec's absence for ten or fifteen minutes. Moreover, if he had delayed his second visit until midnight or later he would have shortened the time during which Isobel was perched on the chair but alive and able to talk and thus the risk of her premature discovery.

I drove on to Strathwood very thoughtfully indeed. If my theory about the way in which Isobel had met her death was correct then the person who killed her grabbed her during that vital few minutes immediately after Gwynne had left for Sydney. That person could have arrived on the car park at the critical time, as I supposed Reeves or Scott had done, or could have been hidden and waiting as I supposed the Thatchers had done. Come to think of it Scott could have done exactly what I had theoretically ascribed to Alec—left Isobel tied up in the store shed and returned later. He had admitted coming back later, a little later it was true, but in fact later.

By the time I reached Strathwood I was deep in the mire again. I had some lovely theories but actually I was hardly any better off than I was when Lindon started on the case.

I still had three major suspects but little hope of pinning the murder on to any one of them. As a matter of fact, I suddenly realized, I had four, counting the Thatchers as one. Rodney Fuller left Strathwood after dinner and was on the car park at some time or other. He claimed to have seen a car leaving and thought it was Scott's but that may have been a cunning statement designed to show that he arrived on the car park *after* Scott had left it. But he too could have come back later. I didn't know when he actually reached the Burnt Gum. It was a mess. The trouble was that exact knowledge of one person's movements depended on statements made by others and the whole damned lot of them could have been lying. If Scott had told the truth for example then either the Thatchers or Reeves were guilty.

Strathwood looked very calm and peaceful in the sunlight when I reached it. A couple of families were evidently staying through the week as a few small children were playing by the pool. I made my way to the back of the building looking for Mr or Mrs Pearce. I was still debating in my mind how to question them without coming into conflict with their loyalty to Alec Reeves when Mrs Pearce came out of the kitchen and immediately started a conversation that eventually solved my problem.

'Oh, Mr Gray,' she said, 'I'm glad you've come. I was going to ring you.'

'Oh? What about?'

'I want to know what to do with Mrs Gwynne's things.'

'Her things?' I was mystified for a moment.

'Her clothes. They're still in the cabin. It's a holiday week-end next week and I know Mr Reeves wants to use that cabin. We are going to be packed out.'

'Have you got anywhere you can store them for the time being?' I asked her.

'Oh yes. That's no trouble but I didn't want to move them before asking if it was all right.'

'It's all right as far as I am concerned, Mrs Pearce. Just stow them away somewhere and I'll get Mr Gwynne to come and pick them up.'

'Thank you, Mr Gray.' She hesitated. 'I suppose you haven't found out who killed that poor woman?'

'Not yet, I'm afraid. We are not even sure where she got to when Mr Gwynne left. Nobody seems to have seen her.' I smiled. 'But you couldn't help me out there of course.'

She laughed.

'We don't have time to see ourselves on Saturday nights. Dinner's always a bit of a scramble when there's a crowd here. But Mr Reeves is very good, I'll say that for him. He's not above giving us a hand in the kitchen when we're rushed.'

'Oh yes. I thought I saw him making for the kitchen that Saturday night just before seven. I suppose he was going to help with the washing up.'

She laughed again.

'He sometimes does even that but he didn't that night. He came to see me about Sunday's meals. It was a few minutes after seven though.'

'Oh?'

'Yes, you see we use the leftover meat for Sunday's salads but sometimes there's a rush on the chicken or the roast beef and we have to substitute something else. It's a bit of a problem because we never quite know how many people are going to be here.'

'I see. Mr Reeves takes an active interest in your side of the business then?'

'My word yes, he's quite fussy. He usually pops into the kitchen after dinner on Saturday to make sure everything's all right and to check Sunday's meals.'

Having got what I wanted, I was about to leave and take a stroll down to the store shed when Mrs Pearce detained me again.

'There's one thing, Mr Gray. I wonder if you could

spare the time to talk to Stan, the stable-boy?'

'Of course. But what is it about?'

'Well you know Jenny Walters told you she heard Mrs Gwynne talking to Mr Scott that Saturday afternoon? The staff are still talking about this, you know, I suppose it's exciting to them. Apparently Stan heard the conversation too and he's a bit worried that he didn't tell you. We all said it didn't matter but you would set his mind at rest if you talked to him. I really think he believes he might be arrested at any moment.'

I laughed.

'I wish everyone was as anxious to talk to us. Where is he?'

'Don't you bother. I'll get one of the girls to find him and send him in.'

'Tell him to come to the store shed, I'm going down there now.'

I'd met Stan of course. He was a shy boy, about eighteen, mad about horses and as fussy about Alec's string as he'd be with prospective Melbourne Cup winners. I didn't expect to hear anything of interest from him but confirmation of evidence is always useful in the presentation of a case, if it ever got that far. But I was wrong.

Stan approached me nervously as I stood near the store shed. I grinned at him.

'Hello, Stan,' I said cheerfully. 'How are the horses? Are you keeping a sharp eye on Corsair?'

'He's going great. That gallop you gave him did him a lot of good.'

'Fine. I hear you have something to tell me?'

'Should have told you before, Mr Gray.'

'Don't worry about it. It's up to me to ask the right questions and if I didn't it's my fault. You heard Mrs Gwynne talking to Mr Scott that afternoon, I understand?'

Stan nodded.

'I heard them.'

'Where were you?'

'Walking up the path from the stables with Mr Gwynne.'

My interest was suddenly aroused.

'You were with Mr Gwynne when you heard the conversation?'

'Yes. I'd been seeing the last of the riders off and Mr Gwynne was down at the stables. We walked back together and when we got to the top of the path I went to the staff building and he went to his cabin. At least, I suppose he did.'

'Let me get this straight, Stan. You walked up the path past where we are now and when you reached the end of the car park you turned right and Mr Gwynne turned left. Where were Mrs Gwynne and Mr Scott?'

'I didn't see them, I just heard them. In the trees.'

'Near the drying yard?'

'That's right.'

'Did you hear what they said?'

'No. I mean I didn't listen. I just heard 'em as I turned round the back of the car park.'

'You recognized the voices though?'

'Oh yes. I did that.'

I smiled.

'Well thanks, Stan. You were quite right to tell me. I'll be coming back here again one of these days and you can have Corsair ready for me.'

He grinned widely.

'I'll be in that. He's a good horse, that one.'

He went off as pleased as Punch leaving me more puzzled than pleased. If Stan Ridge heard and recognized Isobel's and Scott's voices Gwynne most certainly did. On his way to his cabin he would have passed a shade nearer and been within hearing longer than Stan and unquestionably he'd know his own wife's voice when he heard it.

If he'd stopped and listened to his wife teasing Scott pro-
vocatively about going to bed with him and revealing that
she had already done so and would do so again if she felt in
the mood . . . hell, that was enough to make any man angry.
Yet he'd put over that sob-stuff story about his wife being
an innocent fun-lover. Added to what Mrs Thatcher told
me this was surely proof that he had a hell of a strong
motive. He must have murdered Isobel. It just had to be
him. But how did he find the time? Even if he'd raced as
fast as the Jaguar would take him he couldn't have saved
fifteen minutes, not on a busy highway on a Saturday night.
I was sure he couldn't have staged that elaborate scene in
less. He would have been working in semi-darkness and
some parts of his job just couldn't be hurried. Tying that
twine to Mansell's car, for instance.

I unlocked the store shed door and went in. I looked out
of the small window. There would have been some light
coming from the lamp on the corner of the car park and at
ten minutes to seven there would have been some twilight
left. There would have been light enough if he had placed
all the items he would have needed where he could find
them easily.

But it was no use my indulging in wishful thinking.
Gwynne had to meet that plane at eight-thirty, his alibi
depended on it. Eight-thirty? Suddenly I closed and locked
the store shed door and dashed over to the house. I found
Mrs Pearce and asked her if I could use the phone in Alec's
office. She opened it up for me and I grabbed the instru-
ment and rang Trans Australia Airlines. I had to argue the
point a bit and use my police authority but eventually I got
on to someone who could answer my questions. I heard the
replies with a sense of excitement. Yes. All T.A.A. planes
were running a little late that evening. There had been a
minor mishap at Essendon airport and the plane due at
eighty-thirty in Sydney had arrived sixteen minutes late. I
didn't know whether Gwynne's client had travelled by

T.A.A. or Ansett Airways but my next question solved that problem.

'Were all planes leaving Essendon late that evening?'

'Oh yes. They caught up a bit later but the early evening planes were all about fifteen minutes behind schedule.'

Australia has what is known as a two-airlines system for domestic travel. For some reason the airlines despatch their planes within minutes of each other so if T.A.A. planes were late so were Ansett's. Gwynne therefore had fifteen minutes up his sleeve. But did he know that? The only phone available to guests was in Alec's office so he would know if Gwynne used it that afternoon. I rang Alec in his shop.

'Listen, Alec,' I said quickly. 'This could be important. Did Neville Gwynne make any phone calls on the afternoon of his wife's murder?'

Alec answered at once.

'Oh yes, he did. He rang T.A.A. to check the arrival time of the plane he had to meet.'

'Thanks, Alec. Can't talk now but you've helped solve a problem. See you later.'

I rang off. I had the cunning devil. It was a brilliant piece of planning on his part. The moment he knew that plane was going to be late he set up his equipment in the store shed. At ten to seven or thereabouts he left the house with Isobel and went with her to the car park. Once there he didn't waste any time but whipped the gag across her mouth and carried her to the store shed. Ten seconds would have been time enough for that.

His next step? I had to think a bit carefully about this. I said goodbye to Mrs Pearce, got into my car and started to drive to town. Though I was anxious to get back to Headquarters and start the wheels turning I was even more anxious to arrive with a coherent theory to put before Inspector Lindon so I drove slowly, thinking hard. A little after ten to seven then Gwynne was in the store shed binding Isobel's wrists and ankles. His car was still on the car park so there was a danger that someone would see it there. Also there was a danger that someone would see him driving away fifteen minutes later. But would Gwynne have considered those things a danger? There were between fifteen and twenty cars parked together; who would notice that his car hadn't gone. In the ordinary course of events no one would have been around the car park at that hour and he didn't know that Scott was going to leave Strathwood. No one in the house would have shown any interest in the fact that he left later. He could have been arguing with Isobel or going back to his cabin for something. With everyone busy about their own affairs no one would have noticed whether he left at once or later. So he must have proceeded with his task. But how did Scott miss seeing Gwynne's car? He was actually on the car park. There was a simple explanation. Scott wasn't looking for a car but for Isobel. A glance would have told him that she wasn't there. Then, since he was supposed to be returning immediately to Sydney, he drove off without any further attention to his near surroundings. When he had parked his car out of sight and come back on foot he didn't go anywhere near the car park or store shed, he went to Isobel's cabin, approaching it from the trees behind it, so Gwynne was able to prepare Isobel for her eventual death without interruption.

That seemed to explain everything neatly, I thought. When Rodney Fuller turned up on the car park a little later Gwynne had finished his work and it was his car that Fuller had seen disappearing down the drive, not Scott's. I made a mental note to find out what sort of car Scott drove and whether it looked anything like a Jaguar.

I had it wrapped up, as they say in the books. There were no loose ends. Only one thing worried me a trifle. Gwynne's plan had been imaginatively conceived and carefully carried out. In other words it was the work of a man calmly in control of his faculties, not that of one in a manic fury; then why had he let down so suddenly and torn off Isobel's clothes? Besides, he didn't have time to waste and the process must have occupied him several minutes for no gain at all. In the more robust thrillers villains rip off the dresses of heroines as if they were made of tissue paper but having torn up a few old shirts to add a final lustre to the polish on the car I knew that sewn and hemmed material doesn't tear that easily. Isobel's dress had been wrenched and split, shreds of it remained on her arms where the sleeves had parted from the bodice. Her brassière strap had been snapped and the elastic of her panties stretched deliberately to breaking point. Even her stockings had been torn. Why use up valuable time when panties, suspender belt and stockings could have been gently slid down in a quarter of the time? Our original belief that the stripping was a symbolic attempt to expose a faithless body by a man in a frenzy of anger didn't quite square.

Nevertheless, I was convinced that Gwynne had murdered his wife. Everything pointed to it. His motive, his lying, his careful use of taxis to build up his alibi, even his patient wait on the Sunday for the body to be discovered. Perhaps the sight of his wife bound and helpless before him triggered off a desperate urge to humiliate her by stripping her naked before she died. I stepped on the accelerator.

I was back at Headquarters before lunch. Uncle Bob, as usual, was more interested in food than in my theories but he gave in resignedly and listened. I managed to convince him I was right.

'Gwynne murdered her all right,' I concluded. 'It just has to be him. Everything fits too perfectly for it to be otherwise.'

Lindon nodded in agreement.

'There doesn't seem to be much doubt about it,' he admitted. 'But we have to prove it, you know. That isn't going to be easy.'

'But that plane was late . . .'

'So what? He'll say he was there waiting. How can we prove that he got to Mascot only just before the plane got in, with hundreds of other people waiting too? Worse still, how can we prove that he fixed up all that rigmarole before he left Strathwood?'

'We've got enough to shake his confidence.'

'Maybe we have, depends on how tough he is. If he sticks to his story he's going to be hard to break. I'll tell you what we'll do, we'll ask him to come in here this afternoon.'

'If we do that he'll clear out.'

'That would be a damned good thing. It might save us having to rely on all this complicated business with bits of string. If he skips he's guilty and that's the end of it.'

'All right. Will you ring him or shall I?'

'I will. It might sound more forbidding coming from an Inspector though, heavens knows, I'm a mild enough character.'

So he was . . . as a rule. But he could be very, very tough if he wanted to be.

GWYNNE arrived at Police Headquarters promptly at three o'clock and was at once shown into Inspector Lindon's office where Lindon and I awaited him. Lindon set the ball rolling without any delay.

'Well, Mr Gwynne,' he said, 'as you've no doubt guessed this is a further step in the inquiry into your late wife's death. We'll start by going over your evidence again. You left Strathwood on the Saturday night at about ten to seven. Is that right?'

'I'm not going to argue about a minute or two but it was roughly that.'

'Good. And you arrived at Mascot when?'

'A bit after eight-thirty-five I suppose. Say eight-forty.'

'You were to meet the eight-thirty plane so you were late by a few minutes?'

'No. I was early. The plane was late.'

'You knew it was going to be late?'

'Yes. I rang to check the time of arrival before I left Strathwood.'

I knew the smooth bastard was lying but already I saw the force of Inspector Lindon's warning. It was going to be impossible to prove conclusively when he got to Mascot. I was willing to bet he arrived only just in time to meet the plane.

'Where was your wife exactly when you left her?'

'I've already told you that. She was standing on the car park.'

'What did you believe she was going to do after you left?'

'Do? Why, go to the party, of course.'

'You didn't believe she was going to bed with Mr Scott?' said Lindon bluntly.

Gwynne's control was excellent but he couldn't altogether suppress a slight start when he heard this. He didn't speak.

'Come now, Mr Gwynne,' said Lindon. 'Didn't you have some reason to believe that your wife had been carrying on an affair with Mr Scott?'

Gwynne temporized.

'Look, Inspector. I told you Scott had been hanging around my wife but I felt sure she wouldn't go as far as sleeping with him.'

'Really? I think Sergeant Gray has something to say about that.'

I took my cue.

'On that Saturday afternoon you were at the stables seeing the riders off?'

Gwynne nodded, a little puzzled.

'Then you walked up the path to the back of Strathwood with Stan, the stable-boy?'

'Yes.'

'Now that path ends in a tee-junction, one arm going to the staff quarters the other towards your cabin?'

Gwynne now saw where my questions were leading but he had no alternative but to say yes.

'After you parted from Stan you heard your wife's voice and Scott's. Isn't that true?'

Gwynne compressed his lips but again didn't answer.

'Stan Ridge heard and recognized your wife's voice so you did also. You couldn't have helped doing so. You heard her teasing Scott about going to bed with him. You heard her say she would if she felt like it. Didn't you?'

I expected Gwynne to show some sign of concern, if not fear, but he answered quite calmly.

'All right. I did.'

'So you knew that the moment your back was turned your wife would go off with Scott and sleep with him. You also knew that she'd done that before and that she wasn't the innocent creature you had described to us.'

Gwynne took a deep breath.

'I wasn't going to admit to every Tom, Dick and Harry that my wife had been making a bloody fool of me for years.'

'You'd known about your wife's conduct for years?'

'Of course I had. I'm not blind.'

'Why didn't you divorce her?'

'You cops make everything sound so easy, don't you? The girl couldn't help herself but she was extraordinarily careful not to provide me with evidence. I didn't like the publicity associated with divorce, it wouldn't have done me any good business-wise and in any case I would have had to find some man to carry the can. You know enough about the law to understand that casual hoppings into bed aren't good enough. One has to have reliable witnesses to an actual event.'

I switched my questions.

'You are a close friend of Mrs Thatcher's, aren't you?'

'What's that got to do with it?'

'Only that you lied to us about your relationship with her. You told me you had nothing more than a formal friendship with the Thatchers.'

'Supposing I did?'

'Mrs Thatcher visited your flat with you, late at night and alone.'

'I had to talk business with her.'

'Late at night, after a visit to the ballet and drinks at the Wentworth?'

'You've got nasty, suburban minds. Business is done that way nowadays. For your information I took Mrs Thatcher to dinner too. It just happened that she had seats for the ballet.'

'Why did you lie about her then?'

'I played down my association with her because I didn't

want her dragged into this mess and by the way this conversation is going I was fully justified.'

'Mrs Thatcher has been a friend of yours for some time then?'

'A *friend*, yes.'

The interrogation wasn't going quite as I'd hoped. Gwynne seemed to be very confident and had an answer for everything. I wondered whether I could shock him into a different attitude.

'Mr Gwynne. Although your wife died at about one-fifteen on the Saturday night we have evidence that her murder was set up as early as seven o'clock or seven-fifteen.'

'Set up? What the devil do you mean?'

'I think you know all right.'

'I haven't the slightest idea what you are talking about.'

'Your wife was tied up and gagged, placed on a chair with a strap running from her neck to a beam above her head and a string arranged so that when Mr Mansell drove his car away the chair was dragged from under her and she hanged.'

Gwynne stared.

'I don't follow,' he said.

'I think you do. Your wife was placed in position ready to die while you were still with her . . .'

'I was not. I was on my way to Mascot.'

'You needn't have reached the airport until eight-forty-five so you had plenty of time to do all that was necessary. I suggest you left Strathwood not at ten to seven but at about fifteen minutes past. Of course you were miles away with a perfect alibi when she actually died.'

'You're crazy. Why should I kill my wife?'

'You were furious at her going off with Scott.'

'What damned nonsense. I knew quite well she'd been sleeping with Scott and with other men too.'

'You had a combination of motives. You got rid of a woman who had become an embarrassment to you, you cleared the way for a more intimate association with Muriel Thatcher and you expected to share in her coming good fortune.'

Gwynne looked angry.

'I do know what degree of privilege a detective has but I strongly resent your accusations.'

'You asked for them,' I said shortly. 'You lied about your wife, you lied about your association with Mrs Thatcher, you lied about your knowledge of a business deal that was going to net Mrs Thatcher a fortune.'

'Mrs Thatcher's business deals are nothing to do with you. You ought to know that information about such things is not broadcast to all and sundry. She gave it to me in confidence and I was perfectly within my rights to withhold it from you. Besides, as far as I was concerned the whole thing was tentative and nothing to do with me anyway.'

'You agree that you had a lot to gain from your wife's death.'

Gwynne stared at me boldly.

'I agree with nothing. I've given you my evidence.'

The Inspector signalled to me and I kept silent. Gwynne's final words were a challenge and for the moment I had no answer. Lindon stood up.

'Thank you, Mr Gwynne,' he said.

Gwynne departed without a word.

'I was afraid of this, Doug,' the Inspector said to me after the door had closed behind Gwynne. 'I told you if he stuck to his story there wasn't much we could do. It's a hell of a thing to put before a jury and unless we can tie it to him beyond question we haven't a hope.'

'But he did it, Bob, I'll swear.'

'It looks like it, I admit. But what about the others? Scott for example?'

'Damn it, he was going to sleep with the woman. Why should he murder her? Besides he told Alec he was leaving and paid his bill *before* he went to the car park. He must have expected to meet Isobel and take her away somewhere.'

'If all he wanted was to sleep with her why didn't he do it in her own cabin?'

'Because they might have been disturbed. I think Scott's affair with Isobel must have been carried on during the odd hours when Gwynne was out riding and times like that. This probably was the first occasion he'd had the chance to spend an entire night with her. Maybe he didn't feel like facing Gwynne after that so he arranged to bring Isobel back in the early hours of the morning and then clear off home.'

'Well, couldn't he have brought her back some time before one and murdered her?'

'For heaven's sake why?'

'Because she *wouldn't* sleep with him.'

'Good Lord, Bob, all the evidence suggests that she intended to do just that. It was the whole point of the exercise. She was a nympho. Scott's story hangs together. He didn't find her on the car park because Gwynne was busy with her in the store shed.'

'Aren't we leaving Reeves out of consideration?'

'If Alec did it then Scott's story must be true so the only time Alec could have grabbed Isobel was between the time Gwynne left and the time Scott reached the car park. During that time Alec was in the kitchen talking to Mrs Pearce. I've checked that.'

'But Reeves wasn't bound by time. He could have murdered her later.'

'Then where was she when Scott looked for her? And what did she do in the meantime?'

'Hmm. It's a hell of a puzzle. It looks as if Gwynne did murder his wife. But he's been damned clever about it and right now I can't see how we can pin it on him.'

I didn't either and I was still in a gloomy mood when I saw Pat that night. She came to my flat to cook dinner for me but even that didn't cheer me up. In fact I was so irritated about the whole thing I broke all the rules and told her about Gwynne.

'I'm quite sure Neville killed her,' I said gloomily, 'but I just can't think of a way to prove it.'

'I don't think he did,' Pat said.

'You don't? Why not?'

'I think Duncan Scott did it.'

'Good Lord, why?'

Pat smiled a little oddly.

'Let's call it feminine intuition.'

'Break it down, Pat. This is a murder case. I have to have evidence.'

'Well, he could have killed her, couldn't he?'

'Scott? In an ordinary physical sense I suppose so. She could have been waiting in her cottage for him instead of on the car park and he admits to going there after hiding his car and coming back on foot. But why should he murder the girl? He was going to sleep with her and everything we've heard suggests that she was just as willing as he was.'

'I'm not so sure. He could have murdered her because she wouldn't sleep with him.'

'Oh be your age, Pat,' I said impatiently. 'She was ready to hop into bed with any . . .'

'Wait, Douglas. This isn't only intuition, I do know something about my own sex. It's characteristic of women like Isobel to sleep with a man a few times and then want a change. That is what *makes* her a nymphomaniac. She just couldn't stay with one man for long. If you don't believe me look at her record over the last few months. Don Liverson, Rodney Fuller, Alec Reeves and Duncan Scott. And that's just at Strathwood.'

'But Pat,' I protested, 'that conversation Jenny Walters overheard . . .'

'That could be interpreted quite differently. It could have been Isobel's way of telling Duncan that she'd had enough of him. It's quite possible that she intended to dump him and go to the party to look for someone new. If she had got fed up with him she would have told him so in no uncertain terms. She was like that. She could be devastatingly rude at times. Rude enough and arrogant enough to make Duncan want to murder her.'

'But Pat . . . a man doesn't murder a girl just because she won't sleep with him.'

'You don't know Duncan.'

'But surely . . . all that elaborate charade and tearing Isobel's clothes off . . .'

'It's that that makes me certain it was Duncan.'

I stared at Pat and she stared back at me. I'd never seen her in this sort of mood before. She seemed perfectly serious.

'Just why are you so certain?' I asked her.

She hesitated.

'Give me another drink and I'll tell you,' she said.

I poured a couple of whiskies and gave one to Pat. I was puzzled because she seemed so earnest. I watched her as she took a good sip and looked up at me.

'I wasn't going to tell you about this. It isn't a very pleasant story and I don't come out of it very well myself. But I had quite a nasty experience with Duncan.'

'*You* did?'

'Yes, I did, I'm sorry to say. It was a couple of months ago after a party. Duncan can be very charming when he wants to be and at that time I didn't know him very well. During the evening he paid me a lot of attention, danced with me a lot and was very sweet. It was rather a lively party, everybody had a lot to drink, including me. To put it bluntly I was a little bit drunk. That isn't an excuse; I

173

knew what I was doing, or thought I did. Well, after the party ended Duncan invited me into his room for a final drink. Of course I knew what he meant but I wasn't in the mood to care, I was even a bit excited about it.' Pat paused. 'You mustn't get angry with me, girls do behave stupidly at times and I'm no exception. I even thought it might be fun to go to bed with Duncan though I didn't go to his room with that intention. I thought I could make up my mind when the time came ... if it came. We had a couple of drinks and talked for a while but I gradually got the impression that Duncan had taken my acquiescence very much for granted and I didn't like that. He didn't kiss me or fondle me or show me any kind of affection; I was there to be used when he wanted me. So as soon as I'd finished my second drink I stood up and started to move towards the door. I was about to say thanks for the drink and goodnight when Duncan cut in first and demanded to know where the devil I thought I was going. I told him I was tired, it was late and I wanted to go to bed.' Pat took another drink. 'Perhaps I was a bit abrupt and a little tactless but I wanted him to understand beyond any doubt that I had no intention of going to bed with him. He looked extremely annoyed and said I wasn't going to walk out on him after drinking his liquor and I was to forget all ideas about leaving then and get my clothes off. Naturally I refused but as he had placed himself between me and the door I couldn't get away so we ended up facing one another with him telling me to get undressed and me saying I wouldn't. This sounds horribly sordid, I know.'

'Don't worry about it, Pat. You weren't to blame.'

'I'm not so sure about that. Anyway we stood there arguing for a long time. It was a battle of wills. I think he was determined that I should undress for him as an act of submission. Either that or he wanted to humiliate me for rejecting him. He threatened me with all sorts of dire punishments and called me a tease and a cheat. Eventually I

174

decided I'd have to do something so I made a dive for the door but he grabbed me and we began a stand-up fight.'

'Why didn't you yell for help when it reached that stage?'

'I couldn't do that, Douglas. I was in his room of my own free will and it would have been terribly embarrassing at that hour of the morning. Besides I still thought I could handle him and I did. He had my dress over my head a couple of times and my pants half off but I kicked and punched and scratched him until he gave up and told me to get the hell out of his room. I didn't waste any time, I assure you. He looked so mad that I thought he might hit me so I grabbed my bag and ran.'

'That character needs a damned good punch on the nose.'

'No, Douglas. It was as much my fault as his. If you look at it fairly I was in the wrong. There's a ... what do you call it? A *quid pro quo* about these things. Men are quite justified in getting angry with girls who lead them on and then back out at the last moment. I knew perfectly well what he wanted and he was entitled to believe that I understood; if I wasn't prepared to give him what he wanted I shouldn't have gone to his room. But that isn't why I started to tell you about it.'

'Why did you then?'

'Because I don't think his anger had much to do with sex.'

'For heaven's sake, Pat ...'

'I mean it, Douglas. Look. I don't say he wouldn't have made love to me if I'd been co-operative but once I'd defied him it ceased to be a matter of sex. After that he was out to make me submit, to humiliate me, punish me if you like. Underneath, I think Duncan hates women. Maybe his mother smothered him with too much affection or something.'

'You're not going all psychological on me, are you?'

'I think it's important, Douglas. I believe that's why he

murdered Isobel and why he tore her clothes off.'

I stared at Pat. She had me thinking. The stripping of Isobel before she died was one of the most puzzling things about her murder. No murderer gained anything from it. But Pat went on.

'You see I have a strong feeling that if Duncan had succeeded in getting all my clothes off he would have kicked me out, perhaps naked as I was. He wouldn't have touched me sexually, he would have turned *me* down. The same thing must have happened with Isobel. She turned Duncan down, perhaps brutally. She'd finished with him and told him so.'

'In that case he would have strangled her on the spot surely?'

'Not necessarily. He probably got such a terrible shock that he went off to nurse his bruised ego and think up some horrible way to get revenge. Isn't that what he could have done?'

'You could be right, Pat. There were no marks on her body and she hadn't been raped.'

'Of course not. That's part of my argument. Duncan wouldn't have touched her with a barge pole after she'd had the colossal hide to turn him down. All he wanted was revenge.'

'It fits, Pat. It fits perfectly. Isobel must have waited for him in her cabin ready to give him his marching orders. But wouldn't she have realized that she was asking for trouble?'

'Not Isobel. Her ego was even bigger than Duncan's. She wouldn't have dreamed that Duncan would dare to lay a hand on her.'

'All right. I accept that. So when Scott had gone she stayed in her cabin getting ready for the party. Scott fixed up everything in the store shed then went back, gagged and bound her and carried her over to the store shed. He ran a bit of a risk there but somebody did so it could have been

Scott just as readily as anyone else. After that he had un-
limited time, which is an important point because it was
the sort of job that couldn't be hurried and he had to work
in a very poor light. I must say your theory answers a lot of
awkward questions. Only one thing worries me. Whose car
was it Rodney Fuller saw?'

'Perhaps he was a little earlier than he thought and saw
Duncan's car leaving.'

'That must be it. Possibly Scott hung around on the car
park for a while and had only just driven off when Fuller
arrived.'

'There you are then. You've solved the case.'

I smiled a little wryly.

'*I* have? You did most of the solving . . . if the case *is*
solved. I built up a beautiful theory about Neville Gwynne
but it got us nowhere. It's still valid, as a matter of fact.'

'*Is* it?'

'Of course it is. It fits like a jigsaw puzzle.'

'Not psychologically.'

'You're a bit keen on psychology tonight. Why not?'

'Didn't you say that Neville's motive was financial gain?
Some scheme with Mrs Thatcher?'

'It was in part.'

'Then how do you square it with the tearing of Isobel's
clothes? Murder for gain is surely a cool, calm business.'

'You've been reading too many detective stories. Neville
wanted to get rid of her too, you know.'

'How do you know that?'

'Well a woman like that . . . in and out of bed with one
man after another.'

'But she'd been misbehaving for years. Why should
Neville suddenly decide to get rid of her?'

'Because an opportunity occurred for him to make a
good deal of money and get rid of her at the same time.
One motive reinforced the other. The thing that triggered
it, of course, was his discovery that Isobel was going to

sleep with Scott. That would . . .'

I stopped. I saw the trap before Pat pointed it out to me, as I knew damned well she would. If Neville had murdered for gain then the thing had been planned in advance so his discovery of Isobel's intentions could have made no difference. I couldn't have it both ways. Pat was watching me with a faint smile on her face.

'The psychology has broken down, has it?'

'Listen, Professor Morland. The Scott theory hangs together very well, I admit. But there's no more practical evidence for it than there is for my theory about Gwynne.'

'I still don't think Neville would have torn Isobel's clothes off. It's not the sort of thing a *husband* would do. I don't suppose he was sexually very excited by her after so many years of marriage. It was the work of someone still highly entangled with her emotionally, a jealous and rather vicious lover. That's Scott.'

I remembered Gwynne saying that Isobel wasn't even very fond of sex. Maybe he was speaking the truth then and Isobel wasn't very fond of sex . . . with him. Perhaps Pat was right.

'Let's have dinner, Pat,' I said. 'I'm sick of the damned case. I don't know what we can do about Scott anyway. I'll have to talk to Inspector Lindon in the morning.'

We had dinner. It was very nice. Pat was a good cook. I was just going through my records to choose one to play while we were having coffee when the phone rang. It was Joe Allen, one of my fellow sergeants.

'Uncle Bob wants you down at Headquarters right away, Doug,' he said.

'Oh, for God's sake. What is it? A new job?'

'No. It's still the Gwynne case, as far as I know.'

'What's so urgent about that?'

'I couldn't say, Doug. Inspector Lindon just told me to ring you, that's all.'

'All right, Joe. Tell him I'll be there in about twenty minutes. Thanks.'

'You have to go out, Douglas?' said Pat as I turned away from the phone with a downcast appearance.

'Yes. That confounded Uncle Bob is up to some funny business. He was cunning enough not to ring me himself because he knew I'd ask him questions but I have to go, just the same.'

'When will you be back?'

'I haven't a clue. I could be away hours. But I'll drop you off on my way to Headquarters.'

'Why, darling?'

'Why? Don't you want to go home?'

'Wasn't the bargain that if I cooked dinner you would cook breakfast?'

'Yes but I thought as I had to go out . . .'

'What difference does it make? I'll fix the washing up while you're away. Of course I might be in bed if you're very late.'

'I won't mind that.'

Pat smiled wickedly.

'I thought you wouldn't, you old devil. Off you go.'

I kissed Pat quickly and left and I was back in a little under three hours, just before midnight. Pat wasn't in bed. She was still dressed and watching a late television movie. She switched the set off as I came in.

'You are going to have to go back to school again, Pat,' I said to her.

'School? What for?'

'To do psychology over again.'

'Don't tell me I was wrong about Duncan?'

'You were. Neville Gwynne killed Isobel.'

'I don't believe it.'

'Well, it's true. But you were right in a way.'

'How could I be right if Neville did the murder?'

'It was Neville's idea that Scott would be blamed so he

must have agreed with you that Scott's guilt was psychologically possible. But there were three of them in it: Neville and the two Thatchers. My guess is that dear Muriel supplied the brains.'

'But darling, how did Neville manage it? Wasn't he pressed for time?'

'Neville had all the time in the world, honey, well anyway quite a bit more than fifteen minutes. But I'm not saying another word until I've had a drink. How about making some coffee and I'll go and see about some brandy?'

Pat was itching to know what had happened but I refused to say a word until I'd had some coffee. Then I told her.

'Listen, Pat,' I began, 'I'll tell you what that trio did and give you the explanations afterwards. Save your questions, it will all come clear in the end.'

'Get on with it Douglas, I want to know.'

'Have patience. A few days before Isobel's death Neville Gwynne booked a suite at the Wentworth for a John Archer of Archer Fabrications and Archer was due to arrive in Sydney from Melbourne at eight-thirty on the Saturday. According to his story, Neville left Strathwood that night at about ten to seven, which just gave him time to reach Mascot and meet the plane if he drove fairly fast. Now note this. On that Saturday evening Brian Thatcher drove to Mascot and left his car on the car park. He then marched into the airport building, timing his arrival as if he'd just got off the Melbourne plane. Neville in fact didn't leave Strathwood at ten minutes to seven, he left at about fifteen minutes past and it was his car that Rodney Fuller saw. Fuller assumed that it was Duncan Scott's only because he believed that Neville had left much earlier. The point is that Neville had an additional twenty minutes up his sleeve, ample time to take Isobel from the car park and fix her up in the store shed . . .'

'But supposing somebody saw Neville driving off at . . .'

'Don't interrupt. Neville took a chance but I dare say he had an excuse ready and he didn't expect his times to be checked in detail. His real alibi was for the time Isobel died and he was miles away then. So he picked up Thatcher about fifteen minutes to nine and took him to the Wentworth where Thatcher booked in as John Archer from Melbourne. The rest of the story is just as Neville gave it in his evidence except that the whole time Thatcher pretended to be Archer. Neville took him to the Silver Spade, brought him back by taxi and had a few drinks with him before leaving to go home to his flat at Point Piper. All this rigmarole was to substantiate Neville's alibi. On Monday morning when Inspector Lindon rang the Wentworth to check Neville's alibi Thatcher answered him as Archer and confirmed that Neville had picked him up at Mascot when the Melbourne plane came in. The fact that the plane was late proved difficult for Neville because he wasn't able to persist with his original plan which was to arrive at Mascot at about eight-forty-five and have Thatcher swear that he was on the tarmac at eight-thirty. It was the fact that the plane was late that gave me the idea that Neville might have arranged Isobel's murder after all.'

'Wouldn't it have mucked the whole thing up if Isobel had decided to go with Neville?'

'It might have been awkward if she'd made it known that she intended to go but Neville was fairly safe in assuming that she would refuse. She invariably refused and he knew that she was having an affair with Duncan Scott. She wouldn't have passed up an opportunity to be alone with Scott. Neville's main problem was to get her on to the car park but even there he felt sure that she would see him off if only to help discourage his suspicions. I dare say she was quite good at playing the dutiful wife when it suited her. If she hadn't he would have invented some reason for asking her to come to the car park, by telling her he had something important to say to her, for instance. As a matter of fact the plan was based largely on her affair with Scott. Had she not been murdered she would undoubtedly have spent the night with him and we were to have learned of this possibility during our investigations and regarded Scott as our number one suspect. Neville planted this idea in our minds right from the beginning. At the time he didn't know that I was a policeman and had already discovered Isobel's affair with Scott so it was a shrewd move. Now you can ask questions.'

'There's the obvious one, Douglas. Wasn't it terribly risky for Brian Thatcher to pretend to be Archer?'

'Not as they saw it when they devised the scheme. The plan hinged on the fact that we were to be confronted with the body of a woman who had died during the early hours of Sunday morning so the strength of Neville's alibi was concentrated on the later part of Saturday evening. When he took Thatcher to the Silver Spade he deliberately used taxis so he could leave an incontestable record of every minute of his time. The reason Thatcher behaved as Archer was first of all to give Neville an excuse to go to Sydney and secondly to provide confirmation of Neville's movements.'

'It was still a risk, wasn't it, darling? Someone might have recognized Thatcher.'

'The risk was very small. It wasn't intended that Thatcher should come into the picture at all, except as Archer. Because the taxi business was so watertight they expected that any check by us with Archer would be a routine matter and they were quite right, it was. Lindon telephoned the Wentworth and was quite satisfied with Thatcher's statement. At that time the Inspector wasn't particularly interested in where Neville was at eight o'clock, only in where he was at one o'clock in the morning. Like most murderers they were confident they'd been extremely clever. They didn't anticipate that our inquiries would eventually extend to the Bird Cage and the financial dealings of the Thatchers. They imagined we'd still be chasing around after one of Isobel's lovers.'

'I don't quite understand why the Thatchers were in it at all. Why did they involve themselves in Isobel's murder?'

'I think that Muriel Thatcher was at the root of it. She wanted to marry Neville and she wanted to make a fortune, and Isobel's murder offered her a way of doing both. When the sale of the Bird Cage was through the takings were to be divided up between the three of them with Muriel getting the lion's share. Brian Thatcher was just as anxious to leave Muriel as she was to leave him so he was quite content to take a few thousand and get out. Later, either Brian or Muriel would provide the evidence for a divorce so Muriel could marry Neville and live happily ever after . . . they hoped. Neville, I think, had been wanting to get rid of Isobel for some time but had been unable to get evidence good enough for a divorce court. He complained about this to Lindon and me on one occasion and in this instance he was probably telling the truth. As you suggested, Isobel never stuck to one man for long and consequently Neville was never able to catch her in the act with any one man. She chose her moments well, I dare say. So this, coupled with the chance of sharing in a sizable fortune with dear Muriel was enough to make him murder his wife.'

'How on earth did you manage to find all this out?'

'Well, it was Inspector Lindon's work mainly but some of the things I had discovered paved the way. The three of them had some bad breaks. For example, if I hadn't seen that Chaplin film I wouldn't have worked out how the murder had been done. That was sheer luck . . .'

'What nonsense you talk, darling. It was terribly clever of you to solve that. I'll bet Inspector Lindon couldn't have done it.'

'You can be my public relations officer. At any rate it was luck that I saw the film. Their second bad break was that I got interested in the financial affairs of the Bird Cage. That was largely Muriel's fault. I distrusted her on sight and she encouraged suspicion by being so damned cagey. Had she been open and friendly I might not have pushed the thing so far because I'd only started investigating her activities because we were stuck on the sex angle. Another thing was that her story didn't quite match Neville's. He claimed to know nothing about his wife's misbehaviour and nothing about the sale of the Bird Cage to Kenworthy's. Muriel made him a liar in both cases. Then we saw them together and Muriel go into Neville's flat. That was enough to suggest a strong link between them and the possibility that Muriel was somehow involved with Neville in Isobel's death but none of the evidence alone was sufficient to convict them. It took Uncle Bob to finally clinch the case.'

Pat sniffed.

'I'd like to know how *he* managed it.'

I smiled.

'It was just one of those things. Sheer chance again. It's surprising how often little things lead to the solution of a case. This afternoon Lindon happened to be talking to one of his cronies in the Fraud Squad, Inspector Ronaldson. Ronaldson knew of our interest in the Bird Cage because earlier I'd asked his department whether they had any information about it and talking to Uncle Bob he just mentioned casually that Kenworthy's had just announced that they had completed arrangements for the purchase of the Double Bay block and would shortly be building a massive new store on the site. But note this, Pat. Ronaldson didn't tell Lindon this because he thought it would be of any use, it was purely a chance remark. But it was enough to set Lindon thinking, largely because Ronaldson had also mentioned that Kenworthy's had paid a record price. What got under Uncle Bob's skin was that he had worked hard all his life for a miserable superannuation and this bunch had made a packet without lifting a finger. Then he remembered that both Muriel and Neville had claimed that the sale was no more than a vague possibility yet here it was complete. He also remembered that Neville had lied about his relationship with Muriel. He implied that he hadn't known her very well when in fact our evidence, yours and mine, proved that he knew her very well indeed. All this suggested to the Inspector that Neville might have been mixed up with Muriel in some scheme to share in the spoils. This was a motive Uncle Bob could understand. No psychological nonsense, just getting rid of Isobel in order to make a fortune. Lindon is a persistent sort of bloke. Despite Neville's ironclad alibi Lindon took another look at it and suddenly realized that he hadn't paid too much attention to the precise time Neville had picked up his client at Mascot. He had simply assumed that it was when the plane came in. It hadn't seemed very important at the time but now it could be crucial. So Uncle Bob put a call through to Melbourne, Archer was now supposed to be back there, and asked the Victorian Police to get a detailed statement from Archer. Because by this time it was after half past five the Victorian Police had to chase up Archer at his home address and they had some difficulty in finding it. Naturally, because there is no such person. However, they eventually located one of the firm's directors – it's a real firm, a well-known one – and he told them that there were now no Archers in the business, the last one had retired years ago and his name had been Joseph, not John.'

'I told you they ran a risk.'

I grinned.

'It's easy to be wise after the event. Anyway Lindon decided that someone must have impersonated Archer and the only person known to us who could have done that was

Brian Thatcher. That meant that Muriel and of course Neville were all in the plot together. Lindon then had all three pulled in and sent for me. A constable and I took Thatcher down to the Wentworth; because it was at night the same staff were on duty and Brian was immediately identified by several people as Archer. That settled it. I took Thatcher back to Headquarters and we put them all through the hoop, a really tough interrogation. Bit by bit they gave one another away and we got the story.'

'What will happen to them, Douglas?'

'That's up to the Crown Prosecutor. Probably Neville will be charged with murder and the others as accessories.'

Pat frowned.

'You know I could have sworn that Duncan Scott killed Isobel.'

'You were probably right . . . psychologically.'

'Don't rub it in.'

'I mean it. If Isobel had turned Scott down he might well have murdered her. That bunch banked heavily on our suspecting Scott. *That* was why Neville stripped Isobel's clothes off.'

'I see. Then I wasn't very far wrong. You are going to find things a bit tame now that this is all over, aren't you?'

'I've still got plenty to do, mostly paper work. But I might take a short holiday at the end of the week.' I looked at Pat. 'Do you think you could get a few days off?'

Pat stared in surprise.

'Me? I suppose I could. Why, Douglas?'

'I have some leave due to me. I thought I might spend a week at Strathwood, riding and so on. How about coming with me?'

'What a marvellous idea. I'd *love* to.' Pat smiled at me. 'You know you can be quite clever when you set your mind to it.'

'Oh,' I said modestly, 'I'm not bad . . . psychologically.'